Journey into the Interior

Sylvia Moody

Cover by Økvik Design

Published by Broadpen Books,
St Albans, Hertfordshire, UK

It was of course my soul in its
ultimate essence that I had reached.
In many ways I had been its enemy, but
I found it waiting for me as a friend.

Oscar Wilde, *Letters*

Dramatis Personae

Emily Wentworth, a translator

Eileen, a friend

Muriel, a home help

Ira, an angry neighbour

Lachryma, a sad neighbour

Pavida, a timorous neighbour

Pudora, a shy neighbour

Comita, a body related to Emily Wentworth

A blue vase

An image of God

Day 21

Three weeks have passed since the eerie morning when I woke to find that the world was out of focus and my body at a remove from itself. In those three weeks little has changed in my condition except that I'm now composed enough to reflect on my curious situation and strong enough to record at least some of my reflections in my journal.

The phrase 'my journal' perhaps suggests that I'm a habitual journal keeper, but nothing could be further from the truth. Though I've lived a varied and interesting life, I have never felt the desire to record in any detail my doings and feelings, except for a period in adolescence when there was a certain romance in the idea of keeping a diary.

But for many years now I have no more record of the events, inner or outer, of my life than the entries in my appointments diary: 'Dick, 2 p.m. station.' 'Jean, 5. Don Carlo.' '4.30 tea – Aunt Annie.' Such is the written record of my journey through life. Behind these prosaic entries lie fervent passions, bright hopes, deep disillusionments, useful occupations, ecstatic pleasures, desolate wastes and solid joys – but they have not been deemed to merit detailed description or scrutiny.

All the more strange, therefore, that it is only now, in my fiftieth year, at a time when, owing to my condition, my appointments diary is completely blank, when I see no people, do no work, live in nothingness, that it is only now, as I say, that I feel a desire – and more than that – a compulsion to keep a journal.

Perhaps I should begin by describing my condition more exactly. But the curious thing is – that is just what I cannot do. I cannot describe my condition exactly because the very essence of my condition is that it is vague. It began definitely enough with a fever which lasted three days. Since then I've felt myself to be very ill, though, other than weakness, I have no definite symptoms. The only thing I know for certain is that I am not myself – or, more accurately, I am different in relation to the world about me, to the space that I inhabit.

From the first day of my illness – or, as I prefer to call it, my vagueness – my surroundings became unfamiliar and unreal. Household objects, pieces of furniture, pictures, books, vases, all the appurtenances of living that were valued companions, that gave my life a reliable physical structure, these now stand around me like alien presences – austere, brooding, unfathomable silent sentinels. Between their forms lies a silence so profound, a deadness so complete, that at moments I wonder if perhaps I myself have died, that my lifelessness has communicated itself to my surroundings and that my once cherished possessions are in mourning for my life.

My reassurance is the telephone. Occasionally it squawks out in the silence, a sign that I am not in fact dead. I've read about the experiences of people who have temporarily died: they report ethereal lights, long tunnels, beautiful gardens – but not telephones. And those psychic individuals who communicate with the dead rely always on traditional methods – they do not contact the departed telephonically.

So I know I am not dead, but neither do I feel alive. I am not reachable by any of the usual physical and psychical means. True, some rudimentary form of existence continues; each day with greater or less effort I prepare something to eat and drink, perform the usual excretory functions, and wash a section of my body. The rest of the time I doze or stare blankly. From today I shall try to spend a few minutes each day writing this diary, though I fear I shan't have the physical strength to be very regular in this work.

Day 31

My friend, Eileen, came to visit me today. She said she had been telephoning and emailing me for weeks but I never answered. She's down in London for a translators' conference and decided to come over and see me.

Eileen, to my mind, is the sort of person who brims over with life and laughter. She is half-Irish (on her mother's side) and half-English. The Irish in her predominates: she has a mane of red hair, she is open and warm, profligate with words, generous even to those she dislikes – and, on and off, a devout Catholic. When she speaks, her dark eyes, which always have a glint of amusement in them, flash dramatically.

But today even Eileen's natural ebullience was subdued by the heavy atmosphere pervading the room. She sat by the couch, eyeing me doubtfully, the tales of her doings and the saga of her feelings gradually faltering until she lapsed into silence. We sat thus for a while, until eventually I said:

"Eileen, I am becalmed."

I felt surprised to hear myself use that word because I hadn't intended to. I had meant to say something prosaic: that I felt ill, sick, exhausted, depressed. But instead I found myself with a nautical metaphor – especially strange for someone like myself who feels a horror at stepping into even a bath, let alone a boat.

"Becalmed?"

Eileen, too, seemed surprised at the word and she repeated it reflectively. Doubtless we were both thinking of the word's connotations: voyaging, journeying, exploring. We said nothing more of this at the time, preferring to discuss practical matters concerning my care, but, as Eileen prepared to leave, I referred again to my helplessness, saying how stranded I felt, how out of communication with the world.

"Well, start answering your emails", Eileen said. "Or if you're too weak for that, pick up the phone at least. Just make up your mind to rest until you pick up strength. Meantime, you'll have to cultivate your inner life!"

She gave me a kiss and left.

Day 35

Since Eileen's visit I've been giving further thought to her last remark: cultivate your inner life. It sounded like sensible advice, but when I came to think seriously about it, what did it mean really? What was an inner life? A spiritual life? A fantasy life? An alternative reality? A secret life – so secret in fact that it was hidden even from me? Perhaps I had no inner life to discover or to cultivate. Perhaps I would have to create one. And, if I did have one, how could I begin to locate it?

I cast about in my mind for some signpost or clue as to which direction to search in, but I found myself confronting total blankness. Emptiness. Vacuum. Void. Consternation arose within me, and this quickly intensified first into fear, and then into panic. A simple curiosity about an inner life had abruptly tumbled me into nothingness. I felt myself being drawn into this void, pulled relentlessly away from the visible world into a silent universe, into which my whole being seemed to be emptying itself.

I flailed around desperately, seeking some handhold, some hook, which, with its material hardness, would link me back to the world of objects and people. There was none. In a panic I called out:

"Hello, this is Emily Wentworth, of Two Millers Lane. Hello, this is Emily Wentworth, French translator. Hello, this is Emily Wentworth, daughter of Bernard and Mary Wentworth."

At this moment a curious image came into my mind. I saw myself arriving at a grand reception. I was mounting a long flight of steps up to an imposing entrance hall with massive double doors. Through the doors, beyond the puffed importance of a footman, I could see a throng of animated people laughing and talking in a large hall. Light from huge chandeliers flooded the room; the colours of the women's dresses dazzled, and jewellery glinted on their hands and throats. On a table in the centre of the room silver dishes held inviting arrangements of food, rows of glasses sparkled, and a phalanx of bottles gleamed in rich colours.

I became aware of the footman stirring impatiently beside me.

"Who shall I announce, Madam?" he asked.

"Oh – Dr Emily Wentworth," I told him.

He consulted a list. The pause lengthened ominously. Then he looked up with a satisfied nod and said with an air of finality:

"You are not on the guest list, Madam."

"Not on the guest list!" I exclaimed. "But I am the Guest of Honour, the Speaker."

The footman consulted his list again.

"Not according to this, Madam," he replied. "The lecture by Dr Wentworth has been cancelled. She has been reported missing."

"But I am *not* missing," I protested. "I am here."

"Madam, please, regard yourself. You cannot hope to be taken for Dr Wentworth dressed like that. Now, please be off before I call the police. Impersonating a distinguished person is a serious matter."

I was about to protest that I was quite properly dressed when I noticed that I was wearing only a nightdress. A pink nightdress with blue and white flowers on it. I recognised it instantly as the first nightdress I had ever worn.

The hubbub from inside the hall was abruptly stilled and the light from the chandeliers dimmed. I could still see shapes moving in the room, but now they were dark, bat-like forms, silently gesticulating, soundlessly laughing.

I drew back, turning away, and stumbled in confusion down the steps. To my horror I saw that the flowers on my nightdress were beginning to fall off onto the ground and that the pink colour of the material was draining away. The nightdress had turned into a sheet which I clutched to me in a distraught and compulsive fashion as I stumbled along.

My strength, too, was draining from me: my arms and legs became heavy, and a deep humming, like the noise of an angry swarm of bees, grew loud in my head. Gradually my stumble turned to a shuffle, and before long I had sunk to my knees. I crawled along until this too became too much effort and I began to drag myself along the ground. Finally I could go no further: I lay exhausted, my remaining energy dissipating in sobs.

Day 41

The nightmarish fantasy of my repulsion from polite society has remained with me for several days. What I have felt is the cruelty of it. I had started out that evening with the best motives, the best intentions – to offer something useful to my fellow guests – and with modest hopes of enjoying myself. But this had all come to nothing. I had been turned away, denied access and acknowledgement. I had staggered off into the night like a wounded animal, and the party had continued, impervious to my sufferings, ignorant of my very existence.

"Hello, I'm Emily Wentworth, your Guest Speaker …"

I could still hear my last desperate whispering call dying in the silence.

Since that humiliating evening, I've been constantly

exercised by the question of whether I exist or not. Having written this sentence I initially felt some reassurance. There must be a 'me' to be preoccupied with questions about me. I think about me, therefore I am. But I immediately became dissatisfied with this deduction. Thought was not enough. It was too ethereal, too abstract. I pictured clouds of thought floating somewhere above me, fragmenting into kaleidoscopic shapes, forming and re-forming logical patterns. Quite a dazzling display, but I felt no connection with it.

As so often in the past few days, I recalled Eileen's remark: "You will have to cultivate your inner life". If my thoughts were floating above me, what could be inside?

At least, I reminded myself, I must have a physical existence: I had a shape, a solid form. But, as I stared down at my body, that too became foreign to me. I could see that I was connected to it because I could order parts of it to move and they moved. But I felt like a showman pulling the strings on a marionette. Jerk a leg, twitch an arm, shake a foot. A hollow entertainment.

There seemed no way of bringing together the wooden body on the couch and the buoyant thoughts that strutted and danced around the room. In their different ways they were both dead.

A desperate desire arose in me for some token that all was not lost, that somewhere between the lifeless body and the empty coruscating thoughts something lived. I felt I must look further inside myself to find something alive. The phrase 'breath of life' came to me and gratefully I let my mind rest upon it.

In the silent room a faint stirring of air now drew my attention. My breathing. I became aware of the rhythmical rise and fall of my chest, felt the chill touch of the air as it entered my nose and the warmer rush that was expelled from my mouth. The rhythm lulled and soothed me, and the sighing breaths filled the room until the very walls seemed to expand and contract like a living being.

Then, softly at first, from somewhere beyond the breaths, came a beat, a far-off heartbeat, regular, reliable, insistent. Slowly it came nearer, sounding more loudly, vibrating through my body. The breath and the beat joined together in a simple harmony, a minimalist composition for wind and tympany. With my mind free of thoughts and my body liberated from its boundaries of limbs, torso and flesh, I *became* the breath and the heartbeat.

I spoke out loud to the room:

"This is Emily Wentworth, breath and heartbeat."

What a huge feeling of relief these words brought! There was some starting point then. At some crude physical level at least I was alive. I broke down in tears.

Day 61

10 a.m. I am expecting Mrs Muriel Jackson today. I have received notification from the local Community Office:

'Mrs Muriel Jackson has been designated as your Home Help. She will do shopping, light cooking and cleaning, but not windows. Floors must be washed with a long-handled mop. If you have any queries or complaints, please contact Jane at the Neighbourhood Office.'

I have been feeling anxious about this visit for a day or so. Existential questions have ceded centre stage in my mind to questions of etiquette. First and foremost, how should I address my new helper? Mrs Jackson would seem polite, but perhaps a trifle formal? Muriel would be more casual and modern but perhaps a little too familiar?

I have been pondering the modes of address adopted by various friends who employ cleaning ladies or au pairs. Generally they call their employees by their first names, but are themselves addressed formally by their surnames – at least if they are married; the single ones, though, seem happy to be known by their first names – at least, if they are below the age of fifty. Obviously some complicated equation needs to be done involving age, profession and marital status.

But then I am a borderline case. I am widowed and use my maiden name, and I am just fifty. I'm a translator by profession but I'm not now able to work. My friends are in the main high achievers: they run businesses, operate at the top level of their professions, and, in some cases, control financial empires. Their domestic helpers are people that they employ in the same way that they employ assistants or clerks: good service is expected and rewarded; poor service results in dismissal.

But my relationship with Mrs. Muriel Jackson seems very different. I am not employing her; she has been granted to me. Moreover, I'm dependent on her, at least for food and a clean environment. Not yet for bathing and toileting – shudder away the thought! – but, if my condition deteriorates, that might happen too. You couldn't address someone who wiped your bottom for you as Mrs Jackson – could you? People who did that were usually called Mum.

Undoubtedly, the question of my relationship with Mrs Jackson has taken on immense sociological and psychological significance. The conundrum of it has contributed to my sense of having lost myself. One can only be oneself after all in relation to someone else, and it is proving hard to pin down my relationship to the anxiously-awaited Mrs Muriel Jackson. I am slipping and sliding all over the place. I shall just have to lie quietly and wait to see how things turn out.

5 p.m. The fateful reconnaissance visit has been made. I have been given an identity. I am a harmless eccentric called Emmy.

This is what happened:

Mrs Muriel Jackson came promptly at three. I tottered

to the door and opened it, smiling vaguely. Before me I saw a tall ample-bosomed lady with florid features and long curly black hair. She was wearing a colourful dress of floral design, a leather jacket and black high-heeled shoes. Around her neck hung a cross on a silver chain, and large silver ear-rings dangled from her ears.

"Good afternoon," she said. "Emmy, is it?"

"Er, yes, well, Emily, actually, Emily Wentworth."

"I'm Muriel, your home help. Nice to meet you, Emmy."

We repaired to the sitting room and I sank onto the couch feeling relieved. Muriel and Emmy – at least *that* was settled.

Muriel lowered herself cautiously into a chair and glanced around the room with a practised eye. I wondered what she saw, how she would summarise me. Nervously I awaited her verdict.

She seemed a little uncertain at first, but finally nodded and said with studied casualness:

"Read a lot, do you?"

I nodded.

"Mmm," she said. "I like a good book myself – but I don't get the time."

"Are you very busy then?" I asked.

"Busy – ha!" she snorted. "You're always busy in this job. Can't keep up – there's two strokes and an MS on this road alone. And I've got an Alzheimer's starting next week in Friar's Lane."

"Anyone else with my sort of condition?" I asked with sudden hopefulness.

Muriel glanced at a card she was holding in her hand.

"You're a Fatigue, aren't you?" she said. "I did have another Fatigue last year a few doors up, but she's gone now."

"You mean … passed away?" I tried to keep the terror out of my voice.

"No, no, gone away – she got better and went to Torquay. She was like you – read a lot."

She looked thoughtful for a moment, and then added: "Funny, isn't it? Them books must tire you out."

We both pondered this in silence for a few moments, and then our conversation turned to domestic matters.

Day 71

Fatigue continues. Muriel comes and goes with the regularity of clockwork. Her visits are the structure of my life. If she cleans, it's Monday; if she shops, it's Friday. In between is timelessness – space without time.

It occurs to me that before the 'Fatigue' the opposite was true. Life was time without space. My life was mapped out by appointments, but I had no topographical location. Now, as I lie on my couch, I am very aware of my spatial relationship to every object in the room. In fact my relation to them is becoming more than spatial – it is becoming personal. Each of the objects is starting to become animated, to develop a personality.

One object in particular arrests my attention: the blue vase that stands on the table by the window. It is so particular in its curving shape and its blueness, so essentially a vase. It has become a distinctive presence in the room. I watch the subtle changes in its colour against a lightening or darkening sky, the increase and decrease of its shadow in the sunlight, the shiny glow it gives out in the lamplight.

As the days pass, my relationship to it has subtly changed. No longer do I simply observe and enjoy it, I am beginning to venerate it. As I gaze upon it, it becomes luminous, and a circle of light shimmers around it.

To the other objects in the room I talk in a familiar way but the Vase I now address in a formal manner. I sense that it has some knowledge, some wisdom, that can be imparted to me. I have taken to questioning it about my condition, and have received some oracular responses.

This afternoon, for example, I was feeling particularly low and hopeless, and I felt desperate for some sort of support or guidance about how to help myself.

The Vase was twinkling blue in the sunlight, almost as if it was beaming at me. I gazed at it for a long time, absorbing its light and losing myself in its shape. It seemed gradually to expand until its presence was everywhere: a soft blue calmness and gentleness filling the whole room.

I sat for a long time in this contemplative state, feeling a sense of peace and companionship. When, finally, I stirred and the Vase resumed its normal place and proportions, I addressed a question to it:

"O, Vase," I asked, "How can I recover my life?"

At first there was silence, and I began to fear that after all I was alone. But then, the blueness of the Vase shone out more brightly, and there came a sighing breath. A soft murmur, barely caught, brought the reply:

> "Those who can
> renounce their life
> may live in peace
> and free from strife."

I sat for a long time reflecting upon this. How, I wondered, can one renounce what is already lost?

Day 75

Eileen phoned today.

"Hi!" she said. "At least you're answering the phone now. How are you?"

"Trying to cultivate my inner life," I told her. "How are you?"

"Fine," she said. "But I've no time for an inner life – there's too much going on in the outside world."

"You mean … " I paused, "the usual?"

"Well, yes." Eileen said, "If you call Jean-Claude the usual."

"Jean-Claude?"

"Yes," Eileen said. "French. I met him at the translators' conference. You must get well quickly so that you can come and meet him.'

"I'll try," I promised, and then we began to talk of other matters.

I like to feel I'm helpful and loyal towards my friends, but I have to admit my heart sinks every time Eileen produces a boyfriend. Jean-Claude, I know, will turn out to be like all the others: unsuitable. And when the relationship founders – as it inevitably will – Eileen will want to discuss it with me at length to try to discover what has gone wrong. I wouldn't mind, but the story she has to tell is always essentially the same. Our long discussions and in-depth analyses of the situation have no effect. There is a force of habit there that seems impregnable. In some ways her life is as uneventful as mine.

Day 81

Quel jour! I had an unexpected visitor today: Ira, one of the girls in the ground-floor flat. There are two of them down there, Ira and Lachryma, but usually I don't see them. They keep themselves to themselves. I do hear them sometimes, usually late at night. Ira does a lot of shouting and Lachryma specialises in a penetrating and irritating kind of howl.

I don't know what they do all day. They rarely go out, and they don't seem to work. I used to bump into them occasionally on the stairs, but on the whole I tried to avoid it. They both seemed awkward – they would avoid my eye and mutter a brief greeting; they always seemed anxious to get away and not be caught in conversation. Not that I was interested in talking to them – though sometimes I've wondered why they lead such fugitive lives. Perhaps they have a criminal past, or perhaps they are agents of some foreign power. Whatever they are, I've never sought to know them better.

And now – here suddenly was Ira, paying me a visit! She must have heard of my plight – I have seen her down by the gate occasionally, exchanging a few words with Muriel. I assumed she had come up to ask me if I needed anything but at first she said nothing at all – she just sat, hatchet-faced, on the edge of a chair, glaring around the room. She was tall and bulky-looking, with frizzy fair hair and stern features. She seemed rather frightening. I tried – and failed – to think of something to say to her. I felt very weak, and communicating with the Blue Vase had eroded my everyday social skills.

We remained thus silent for what seemed an age. Ira became increasingly fidgety, and kept darting angry looks at me. Then suddenly – alarmingly – she leapt to her feet and began to pour out a stream of invective:

"Bastards!" she shrieked, "Piss-pots! Ass-holes …"

I could only gape at her. Clearly she had no social skills at all.

She started to march up and down the room. Her face was contorted into a puckering, palpitating ball of flesh, deep within which two fiery orbs glinted and flashed.

"Farts! Turds! Scum!"

The obscenities continued to pour out of her (I don't want to record them all here), and I remained agape.

But she seemed oblivious of me. Her wild eyes stared sightlessly as she continued to shout and swear. Eventually she seemed to run out of obscenities – or perhaps found them wanting – for she abandoned words and began to emit strange growls and howls, low at first but gradually rising to a crescendo.

The bewilderment I had felt about her visit and her behaviour turned to terror. I was trapped with a wild animal. Grotesque thoughts came into my mind: she would attack me, bewitch me, eat me. I was sure that I glimpsed dragon's fire flickering between her lips and her eyes glowed redder and redder. Her howling turned first to wailing, then to shrieking. I sat transfixed with horror as she threw herself down beside the couch, pummelling it with her fists.

Oh, God, I thought, she is going to explode.

Suddenly galvanised, I grabbed hold of her, and, at that moment, she appeared to gain some awareness of me. Her eyes rested on me for a few seconds and it seemed that from somewhere in her tormented mind came a moment of clarity. She grabbed my arm and clung to it, yelling:

"Help me! Help me! For God's sake, help me!"

I was completely at a loss, but my fear left me. I saw that my visitor was in some torment that consumed her entirely; she was not concerned with me, not concerned with either harming or helping me.

A mixture of pity and resentment rose within me. Pity for her plight, and resentment that she spared no thought for my predicament. I was the one who was ill, after all, I was the one who needed help. But she was still clinging onto me, and her nails dug into my flesh.

I cried out in pain, and at that moment her screaming abruptly ceased and she drew back slightly. We sat staring at each other until, on an impulse, I reached out and took her hand in mine.

"What is it?" I asked her. "What is it?"

She made no answer at first. She just sat gripping my hand, her body still heaving slightly as she emitted strangled sighs and sobs.

"What is it?" I asked her again.

I could hardly imagine being of any help with her evidently massive problems, but I thought that perhaps I could just comfort her a little.

She had relaxed her grip on my hand, and, staring me straight in the eye, she said in a clear ringing tone:

"It's them!"

"Them?" I asked, bewildered.

"Them," she repeated. "Them, them, them …"

"Who …?" I began.

She started to shake me.

"Them! You know who I mean. Them. The bastards, the wankers …"

"Please, please," I interrupted her in desperation. "No more swearing. No more screaming. I can't take any more. Please, I can't."

"All right," she said angrily. "You don't want to know. Fine, forget it, just forget it."

She stood up and moved towards the door. Her face was set, resigned, hopeless.

I felt desperately sorry for her. To live in such torment!

"Wait," I said. "Don't go, please. Look, I want to help you, but I don't understand what's going on. And I am ill myself, you know."

She paused at the door, looking at me thoughtfully. Her face seemed to soften slightly.

"Well," she said, "I'm sorry if I've upset you. I know I'm not a very relaxing visitor. I'll come up again when you're feeling better – or when I am."

She gave me a nod and departed. I heard her footsteps thumping down the stairs, and then a door banged.

The silence that followed was oppressive. The air seemed clogged with emotion, suffocating. I lay still, trying to make sense of the sudden tumult that had descended upon me. My body felt unbearably tense. I lay still, trying to relax, but the distress caused by my tempestuous visitor did not leave me.

Day 82

I had a very bad night. Ira visited me again and again in my dreams, and this morning I still felt tense and exhausted. Casting about for some way to calm myself down, I recalled that Eileen had sent me a book on relaxation exercises. I had put it somewhere under the couch. After groping around, I found it and, propping myself up on all sides with cushions, I turned to the first exercise. The instruction read:

'Empty your mind by concentrating on a word or symbol of your choice.'

A word or symbol of my choice. This required some thought.

Presumably I should try to choose something that had few connotations – certainly something with no strong emotional content. I needed a vapid, neutral sort of word, perhaps a preposition or, even better, an article – was there anything more vapid, after all, than the word THE?

I tried repeating it softly to myself: THE, THE, THE. But it seemed unsatisfactory on its own. It seemed to require, if not positively demand, a companion. Hard as I tried to confine myself to THE, it constantly attracted to itself a collection of substantives: THE DOG, THE CAR, THE KETTLE, THE DEMON.

Pictures of these entities in various combinations began to flash through my mind. A dog, a dog in a car, a demon in a car with a kettle. No, this wouldn't do. I should try something that could stand alone and would be difficult to picture, say, a nice abstract noun. I alighted on the word PEACE. I would rest my mind on peace.

PEACE, PEACE, PEACE – Peace comes dropping slow. Yes, that affecting Yeats poem which had such sad associations for me: it had often been recited by a friend who, finding no peace herself, had finally taken her own life. Tears welled up as I remembered her. What demons had possessed her? How could one find peace when others did not?

I recalled that I was supposed to be relaxing, not agitating myself with memories. Meditating upon words was not proving helpful, so I decided to try a nonsense word. This should dispose of associations, I thought. But it proved harder than I had imagined to decide upon a candidate. I wrote down two or three possibles and tried saying them: WISHONY, COLLOROMO, BIGWOLLY.

What hideous creations! The very act of pronouncing them made me wince. And what empty things they were. In repeating them, I felt myself reduced to meaninglessness. Not the bliss of Nirvana, simply the hell of emptiness.

This wasn't working. I closed the book, vowing, however, to try again the next day.

Day 83

Back to the relaxation book. (One thing I'll say for myself is that I don't easily give up.) I leafed through the pages and began to read a section called 'Images'.

'Some people,' I was informed, 'prefer to let their mind rest on an image rather than a word, perhaps a beautiful garden or a tranquil lake.'

Perhaps I was such a person. An image person. It seemed unlikely because I had always been a wordsmith. I described things rather than saw them. I could spend a whole evening at a friend's house and come away with no memory of the clothes she was wearing, the decor of the room, the pictures on the wall. No, I was hardly an image person.

It occurred to me at that moment that I had very little memory even of the picture that hung on my own wall, above the fireplace. It was a seascape painted by a friend, and given to me as a fiftieth birthday present. But beyond knowing it was a seascape, could I really picture it?

I stared at it now, concentrating on the shapes and colours. In the foreground were square little houses, and beyond these a lighthouse, an expanse of choppy sea and a sky with a purple-red swirl of clouds.

It was from the clouds that a startling image suddenly stood out: a bearded biblical face with a frowning expression. It was lost at once in the whirling tumult of the clouds. But a few seconds later it loomed into view again, more thunderous than the sky. There was no mistaking its identity: God was nestling there among the clouds! And from the look of Him, He was the Old Testament God – minatory and uncompromising.

This experience was unnerving. The room seemed suddenly filled with His presence and I felt acutely conscious of His gaze. I stared at the picture, willing my eyes to see clouds, only clouds, but He remained obstinately visible.

What a wretched turn of events! Now on top of everything else I had to have God in the room, obviously disapproving. Probably He had visited me with this illness as a punishment for something.

Day 84

Ever since yesterday, I have remained acutely conscious of God's presence. Anxiety has been growing within me that I have been judged and found wanting in some way. Perhaps I have done something criminal, or committed some act of gross moral turpitude? I feel sure I must have, but I can't recall it. Evidently it is something so heinous that it cannot be entertained even in memory. A crime so execrable that it has been banished to some deep pit, where day and night it writhes and heaves screaming out for condign punishment.

What could it be, this unspeakable sin? I woke in the night and saw around me people standing with averted eyes. Clearly, I was too awful to be contemplated. I had been judged and found guilty, and a life sentence had been passed. But then somehow I had got away – and all my life I had been on the run. Now, finally, I had been apprehended, and would be made to face my crime.

I saw myself being led away. I was taken down crumbling stone steps, along dark corridors, through echoing caverns, down to where silent cisterns gaped, down further to where subterranean streams snickered in dark channels, down, down still further to the black chasm where my crime lay waiting for me. It was to be my companion for the rest of time.

Blackness closed on my soul and I lay rigid. What hope was there? What escape from this torment, this nightmare?

"The Blue Vase! The Blue Vase!"

I cried its name aloud. I must communicate with it, I must seek its help. I must question it.

Sitting up, I turned on the small reading lamp. With relief I saw the Vase was in its usual place, shining with its deepest blue.

"O Vase," my voice came as a whisper from a

great depth. "O Vase, what is my crime? Why am I in torment?"

I waited in the silence, preparing myself for its answer. Then from somewhere close beside me came a sighing breath, and I felt a caress of cool air on my face. The answer came:

"There's damage done
And too much harm.
The one you shun
Sounds the alarm."

A frowning God or a gnomic poetaster. This was my choice.

Day 88

I spent most of the day lying motionless, gazing at the ceiling. Towards evening I revived slightly and looked about me. The room was silent and sombre. The sun had moved beyond the window and the Blue Vase lay in shadow, its blueness deepening into mauve and then black. God had disappeared behind his clouds. There was a soft light in the room, melting and muting the outlines of the furniture. In contrast, the flowers outside in the window boxes caught the rays of the setting sun and gleamed in clear, bright, almost gaudy, colours, turning smiling faces to the evening warmth.

Life and death were both present. What was the

difference anyway? Those plants had but a few weeks to survive. Were they living or dying? And where was I on the continuum? Was I dying, or was I just imprisoned temporarily in a dead landscape?

Day 101

I have been looking at my relaxation book again today. I decided to try the 'Fragrant Valley' exercise. In this I have to think of myself as gradually descending steps on a hillside in a broad valley. On either side are wide terraces with colourful, sweet-scented flowers, shrubs and blossom trees. As I descend lower, the steps become steeper, the terraces narrower. There is bird song in the distance and all around the sound of crickets, a hum of life in the intensifying silence and peacefulness.

I keep going down, down, down into the silence. The path has narrowed to a foot's width and is overhung on all sides with foliage – dense, cool and protecting. I hear the sound of water, and, slithering down the last few yards of the path, I find myself on a delightful grassy riverbank. A broad stream flows smoothly along, and on the far bank lies an expanse of olive and fruit trees.

Looking along the bank on my side of the river, I see a hammock strung between two trees. Here, says the relaxation book, I can recline in perfect peace, letting the river take away the chatter in my brain.

Peace and tranquillity! Eagerly I approach the

hammock, longing to swing there, releasing my thoughts into the passing current.

But then, oh then, o moment of horror! A dreadful sight materialises before my eyes! The hammock is not empty: it contains a creature, a malign, demonic form – an imp, a sprite, a devil. Sneering and cackling, this monstrous being rises up towards me, beckoning, reaching out to clasp me in its serpentine arms.

I hear a scream, a frightful sheet of sound that rises upwards, enveloping the terraces and escaping from the sunken regions, travelling out far beyond the human realm. As I scramble back up the hillside, fleeing from the dreadful valley and its lurking terror, I recognise the scream as mine. I have become the scream.

Day 111

Time has gone by. I don't know how many days I have been lying here. Muriel comes and goes. Occasionally the telephone rings and voices enquire about me. Do I want anything? The real world seems so distant – it's as if beings from Mars are concerned about me. What can I tell these voices? All I want is to be alive, to be human, to return to the world and join the ranks of busy people who walk purposefully up and down the road, on their way no doubt to work or to the shop or to see a friend. I feel that even hospital visiting or a dental appointment would be a treat.

It is such a long time since I walked out in the world. Life beyond this room has become remote and unreal. Occasionally I turn on the television news in an attempt to connect myself to concerns larger than how I am going to cook a meal or get my radio mended. I watch the figures on the screen with bafflement. Often I turn off the sound because the noise disturbs me, and the succession of silent mouthing faces, some earnest, some jovial, some angry, presents a tableau of human life at a remove.

Occasionally when I see a face that looks particularly wise or kind, I stretch out a hand in a soundless plea for help.

Day 120

There was a hesitant knock on the door this morning. I was feeling a little stronger than of late and called out:

"Who is it?"

A hoarse voice replied:

"Lachryma, Ira's flatmate."

"Oh, come in," I called. "It's not locked."

I had been alone for a few days, and felt it would be good to chat to someone – though I wasn't sure if Lachryma was the right person. Whenever I had met her on the stairs, she had always seemed so sad-faced and preoccupied. I thought she might depress me. Still, beggars can't be choosers, as Muriel so frequently remarks. And she surely couldn't be as bad as her tumultuous flat-mate.

Lachryma came in quietly. She looked as glum as ever, and her face seemed puffy and swollen, as if she had been crying. She was wearing a black jogging outfit and a black knitted hat over her lank dark hair. Overall she made a very dismal impression.

She sat on the end of the couch, sniffing slightly.

"Ira said to come up and see you," she said, "but I don't know – I'm not in a very good state myself. I don't suppose I can help you much, but let me know if there is anything …"

"Thanks," I said. "Actually, I'm feeling a bit better at the moment. I was just going to make some tea – would you like a cup?"

"Thank you," she said. "That would be nice."

"I've got some muffins, too," I said. "My home help baked them for me."

For a second, her face lightened; her lugubrious look faded and she gave an appealing smile.

What makes someone so sad, I asked myself as I stood idly in the kitchen waiting for the kettle to boil. She seemed a nice person, and quite healthy. What right had she to be sad? I hoped she wouldn't upset me, just when I was feeling a touch improved.

But, when I went back into the sitting room, I found

my fears realised. Lachryma was sitting hunched in a chair, pressing a dank handkerchief to her face and sobbing. She took no notice of me, so I put the tea things down in front of her and sat down on the couch.

Fine neighbours I had! Fine lot of help they were! So preoccupied with their own problems that they completely ignored my difficulties. I just had to go on heroically coping not only with my condition, but with the condition of those who supposedly came to help me. Ira's fury, Lachryma's sorrow, Muriel's platitudes – what use were they to me? I glared at Lachryma and determined to ignore her sobs.

"Won't you have some tea?" I asked her with the studied politeness of a bored hostess.

She made no reply and her sobs became more violent. Her body shook convulsively and tears poured down her cheeks, spattering into the tea.

"Do you take sugar?" I asked, making my voice calm and neutral.

This seemed to rouse Lachryma to even greater paroxysms of grief. She gave a choking cry and slipped from her chair to the floor where she lay thrashing and writhing and emitting dreadful ululations.

Compared to this, I thought, the Mad Hatter's Tea Party was tea at the vicarage. Who would rid me of these turbulent neighbours?

As Lachryma continued to twist and shriek, I made a further effort to put our encounter on a normal social footing.

"Would you care for a muffin?" I asked.

But I might just as well have been talking to myself. She was lost in her anguish. Unable to contain my rage any longer, I banged down my teacup and yelled at her:

"Have a muffin, damn you! Have a muffin! Stop crying and damn well have a muffin!"

Her sobs abated slightly, but my fury increased. I was tired, ill, helpless, and just one day when I was feeling a tiny bit better, just a smidgeon recovered, I was faced with this lachrymose creature, snuffling and sniffling and sobbing. And rejecting my muffins. I grabbed wildly at the muffins and started hurling them at her.

"Go away!" I screamed. "Leave me alone. I've got enough problems without your misery."

I went on pelting her with the muffins until the plate was empty. She just lay there snivelling while the muffins bounced off her. They rolled around the floor, lodging in odd corners of the room.

Finally she became quiet. I too lay back on the couch exhausted. We remained in silence for a long time. The atmosphere in the room seemed intolerably heavy, as if her sobs had humidified the air. I felt myself gulping for breath.

The silence was broken by Lachryma blowing her nose. She darted me a glance and then said in a conversational tone:

"Well, I'll be off, then. Sorry if I've disturbed you. Let

me know if there is ever anything I can do for you."

She went out. I heard the front door click and the creak of the stairs as she descended to her own quarters. As the sounds of her retreat died away, I began to weep. What else was there to do?

Day 123

I asked myself today: Am I being a victim? Am I letting myself be persecuted by my neighbours? Am I too passive, not assertive enough?

But what can I do? They simply appear without warning from down below and overwhelm me with their troubles. If I weren't ill, I could move to another house, share with some quiet respectable gentlefolk who kept themselves to themselves and saw to it that the hedge was trimmed.

That is another thing: the garden. It distresses me to look out at it. The hedge is a ragged tangle, the lawn a memory, and the flower beds a minor jungle. I long to summon a gardener to tend it, but it doesn't belong to me; it belongs to the two women in the basement.

That there are two women living in the basement is something of a surmise, because I have never actually seen them. However, post occasionally arrives for them, so I know their names: Pavida and Pudora Smith.

What a pair they sound! Why can't I have neighbours

with normal names and normal behaviour? I am victimised by God and Man and especially by my intolerable neighbours.

Day 124

Today I felt I needed more help with this victim question. It was a moment for consulting the Blue Vase. It was in its usual place, a solid, reassuring presence. I thought for a while about the best way to formulate my question, and then said:

"Oh Vase, how can I end this persecution?"

I sat for a long time waiting in the silence. Then came the faintly sighing breath, and the reply:

"Love the pain and hear its cries

Look on it with tender eyes."

Victimised by God, Man and doggerel verse, I drifted off to sleep.

Day 126

Eileen telephoned today, asking if she and Jean-Claude could come and see me. They were in London on a shopping trip.

"Are you any better?" she asked. "Can you manage visitors?"

"I'm sorry, Eileen," I said, "I don't think I can. I'm just too weak to talk."

"You sound weak," Eileen said, sounding concerned. "Are you sure there isn't anything we can do for you?"

"I think I just need to rest," I told her.

To tell the truth, I'd been so weak today I just wanted to get off the phone. It was difficult even to hold it.

"All right," Eileen said doubtfully. "I'll let you rest then. But I'll call you again soon."

Afterwards I felt upset that I hadn't been able to speak to Eileen properly or to invite her and Jean-Claude round. Or at least to think of something they could do for me.

I was so weak and helpless: surely I needed some help. The trouble was: I felt beyond help. Beyond the sort of help that any individual could give me.

I let my eye rest on my harbour picture. Any port in a storm. Before long I saw God's features emerging from the clouds.

Perhaps I should pray. To Him. It wasn't something I would normally have thought of doing. But then what had I to lose? And it might be that I would benefit from some sort of religious placebo effect.

"Dear God," I prayed aloud, "please help me to get better."

But no sooner had I spoken these words than it struck me how absurd it was to imagine that God would be concerned with making an individual better. After all,

He had been presiding over the whole of creation for billions of years, and presumably He had by now struck some balance between what was better and what was worse. If I got better, perhaps someone else would have to get worse. Perhaps I should just accept things as they were. That wasn't being a victim after all, that was being a philosopher.

Day 127

It is so difficult to relax. I have tried all the suggestions in the relaxation book – but all to no avail. Today I decided not to try anything at all but just to lie still and notice how my body was. I was immediately aware of tension everywhere, from my neck right down to my toes. I consciously relaxed my muscles and continued to lie quietly. Then all at once the tension was back again. No matter how often I made myself relax, the tension returned – like an obsessional thought that re-establishes itself as soon as we are off guard.

Impatiently I wriggled my shoulders and spine. Something must be trapped somewhere, and needed freeing. I sighed. Another task …

Day 128

Last night I dreamt about Ira and Lachryma. I dreamt that they went to the reception to which I had been denied entry.

Ira was dressed in a dramatic purple trouser suit with matching platform shoes, and her hair was coiled in a tall confection on top of her head. Lachryma – need it be said – was in a little black dress, with black stockings and knee-length black boots. Her long hair fell untidily about her ever-drooping shoulders.

I watched as Ira swept up the steps to the door with Lachryma trailing listlessly behind her. The aloof footman was at his post. Surely they would never get past him.

"Good evening," Ira said imperiously. "I'm Ira Brown, and this is my friend, Lachryma Jones. We have come for Dr. Wentworth's talk."

The footman gave them an appraising look and consulted his guest list. Now, I thought, let them get the benefit of his *hauteur*.

But, to my amazement, he simply made a couple of small motions with his pencil and said:

"Oh yes – I have you down here. Please go through. Refreshments are on the right and the talk will be in the Assembly Room. But I regret it will be late starting – the speaker has been delayed."

Delayed? What an outrage? I ran to the nearest window and hammered on it.

"I'm not delayed," I yelled, "I'm here! They won't let

me in."

A few people standing by the window glanced vaguely in my direction but were soon engrossed again in their conversation. Helplessly, I watched as Ira and Lachryma made their way across the room to the refreshment table. Their presence evidently caused quite a stir. Heads turned and people pointed towards them, exchanging whispered comments.

Ira stood by the table staring belligerently around the room. A waiter offered her a glass of wine, but she waved it away impatiently. Lachryma in the meantime had furnished herself with a bottle of wine and a large tumbler. She retired to a sofa in the far corner of the room and sat staring dully into space. Soon she began a monotonous routine of filling her glass and draining it.

I wondered if either of them would attempt to socialise. One or two of their fellow guests had made hesitant moves in their direction but had either been waylaid or lost courage. Around the room the murmur of voices rose and fell, glasses clinked, and ripples of laughter broke out here and there.

Ira was still standing by the table, glaring at the assembled company. Then, suddenly, she marched across the room to the sofa where Lachryma was morosely drinking. She snatched the wine bottle and tumbler out of Lachryma's hand and smashed them onto the floor. The buzz of conversation around the room died and the guests stood transfixed gazing at the two women.

"Oh, come on!" Ira shouted. "Come on, let's get out of here. These people are dead from the toes up. I'm not going to any lecture with this lot."

An uneasy murmur ran round the room.

Ira tried to pull Lachryma up from the sofa, but Lachryma resisted.

"No," she said in a loud voice. "I'm sick of you yelling and bossing me about."

"And I'm sick of you crying and getting pissed," Ira shouted. She continued tugging at Lachryma.

"Look, can we help?"

One of the guests stepped forward – an earnest-looking young man who was sporting a bow tie.

But Ira pushed him unceremoniously aside.

"You've had this coming for a long time," she said to Lachryma – and, as a gasp of horror went round the room, she gave her a sharp slap across the face.

"And you've had this coming for a long time," was Lachryma's surprising rejoinder. She kicked Ira on the shin.

Ira then retaliated by tugging Lachryma's hair, and the two of them struggled together on the sofa. The young man in the bow tie threw himself on top of them, trying to separate them, and several other guests joined in the mêlée.

As the footman with a cohort of officials advanced across the room towards the writhing heap of bodies, I fled the scene.

Day 131

Muriel came this morning. Bright-eyed and bushy-tailed, as they say. After humming over the dusting for a few minutes, she asked me:

"Been on your own all weekend, have you?"

"Yes."

After a sympathetic pause, she continued:

"I know what it's like. I used to be my own a lot after the divorce. Couldn't stand it".

Muriel had never mentioned a divorce before – I had always assumed there was a Mr Jackson somewhere in the background.

"Do you still get lonely?" I asked her.

"Too busy," she said. "But, anyway, I'm with another fellah now."

"Oh – that's nice."

"Yes. Met him through my Church. I've known him for years – him and his wife, but last year he was widowed, and, well, time has gone by and we've got together – just recently actually.'

"Congratulations," I said.

"Thanks, love," she said. "All's well that ends well. I hope you'll be as lucky."

The humming started again, but was soon lost in the drone of the hoover.

Day 132

I have been thinking today of the man I married, and the men I perhaps should have married. Since falling ill, I haven't given any thought to men, for the mere thought of them is tiring. Seeking one, vetting one, courting one, satisfying one, expecting things from one, negotiating with one, agonising about one …

I decided to take God to task on this subject. He was still there in the picture, alternately emerging from and merging into the cloudscape.

"Tell me," I asked Him, "how did this idea of two sexes come to you? Is it an experiment you're trying on this planet? Somewhere else in the universe, in some far-off galaxy perhaps, are you trying out other methods?"

Of course, I don't expect any answers, but, really, when you think about it, life on earth is extremely puzzling. Millions of species preying on one another, and billions of individual creatures seeking sex. How did such an idea come to God in the first place? Was there not a more dignified option?

Reputedly, He is a mathematician. For my part, though, I like to think of Him more as a literary type: a novelist – even, on a good day, a poet. He has begun a cosmic tale, and like all good stories it's taken on its own momentum. Even He doesn't know where it will end.

Day 135

When Muriel came today, I was feeling quite ill. I lay staring at the ceiling, my head buzzing, my limbs aching.

Muriel sensed that I was feeling poorly; she gave me covert looks while she tidied up the room.

"What is it, love?" she asked after a while. "Not feeling too good today?"

"No," I said. "Everything's on top of me – this illness, the weather, the neighbours."

"Oh, neighbours!" Her tone was expressive. "Are they being noisy then?"

"It's not so much that – they are just, well, so unpredictable."

"Don't let them worry you," Muriel advised me. "As long as they're not noisy at night. We had that last year – a young couple moved in next door and they played music at all hours. Derek – that's my fellah, love – he soon put a stop to it, though."

"How did he do that?"

"He threatened to kill them," Muriel said with relish.

"Oh really – heavens!"

"So, if you have any trouble with the neighbours, love …"

Briskly, she plumped up the cushions on the couch.

"At least," she said, "you're nice and private up here with your books and your flowers. Count your blessings."

Day 136

I've been thinking about what Muriel said yesterday: count your blessings. Now, there is wisdom for you. When I think what could be happening to me. I could be being burnt as a heretic in the Middle Ages; I could be incarcerated in a vermin-infested prison somewhere to punish me for being democratic; I could be orphaned in a civil war; I could have lost my life to drugs, drink or depression, or met a psychopath on a lonely road.

When I think of all the things that could be happening – that are happening to millions of unfortunates – then what's a Fatigue? What are Lachryma and Ira? What is a little disillusionment with God? And yet I feel I am reaching the end of my tether.

Perhaps what is most difficult to bear about this Fatigue is that there seems to be no obvious reason for it. If one suffers, one feels one should know why; one should be able to see, if not a purpose, at least a cause. Where the Fatigue is concerned, there is no obvious cause. I am not the victim of an identifiable virus, I am not starving, I haven't been working myself into the ground. The problem is somehow in me, in the way I am living, in the way I am conceptualising life. I feel defeated by my condition, but why has my life become my enemy?

Day 139

I was woken this morning by wailing and shouting from the flat below. A bad start to the day. I do like to begin the morning quietly, easing myself gently into wakefulness. It takes my muscles an hour or so to get moving so I just lie peacefully looking at my flowers and making the odd comment to God or the Blue Vase.

I can't tolerate noise at all. It makes me sad because I have always loved music, and now the enjoyment of that has been lost. Even birdsong aggravates me, and every morning I curse a particularly loud warbler who has taken up residence in the eaves.

How much more then did I curse my neighbours now. Their racket was intolerable. So loudly were they yelling that I could hear their words clearly. I tried to turn my mind away from their voices, but suddenly my attention was caught by the sound of my own name.

"Emily, Emily, Emily!" Ira was shouting. "That's all you ever talk about these days. Let the subject drop, for God's sake."

Lachryma's answer came in the form of a loud wail.

Ira's stentorian voice continued:

"Just stop it! You've upset her, okay? I've upset her, okay? We didn't mean to, we've got problems, right? She can see that, she's not too ill to see that."

"She's too ill to help us," came Lachryma's wailing reply. "Far too ill. We should be helping her."

"Us help her? That's a nice one? What has she ever

done for us? All the years she's lived up there and she can barely manage a 'good morning'. Do me a favour, stop feeling sorry for everyone, including yourself."

A long silence followed this and I began to feel hopeful that they had now quietened down. However, I felt disquieted by their remarks. I had no idea that they had been giving any thought to me, or that they had any resentments against me.

As I was pondering this, I became aware of a low moaning sound which seemed to be coming from the flat below. Growing in intensity and plangency, it rose up towards me through the cracks in the floorboards until it completely filled my room. I tried to close my ears to it but it penetrated my whole body. I could find no refuge.

Then, from somewhere beyond the moaning, came another, terrifying, sound: a shrill screaming, distant at first, but gradually approaching nearer. It was the shrieking of Furies, of wrathful creatures, a murderous hate-filled howling. It entered my body like a dagger, tearing me, gutting me. I writhed in torment.

Suddenly, from the heart of this infernal cacophony, a clear sound rang out: an insistent ringing. At first it seemed that this sound, too, was within me, but gradually it became more separate. It grew louder and louder, and the moaning and screaming died away. Eventually I realised that the ringing came from the telephone.

Dazed, I picked up the receiver, and gave a whispered "Yes?"

"Emily!"

I recognised Ira's irate voice at the other end of the line.

"Emily, please, can you stop making that racket? We can't hear ourselves think down here."

The line went dead and for the rest of the day profound silence reigned in the house.

Day 140

Yesterday was very confusing and upsetting. I've tried to make some sense of it but I feel too drained and exhausted to think properly. I've certainly been very quiet today – and so have my neighbours. Perhaps we are all feeling chastened.

I do wish I knew better how to deal with them. I feel sure they must need some help in coping with the violent emotions that grip them. At the moment they just seem to be putting them into me!

Still, things could be worse – I could be sharing a flat with them.

Day 141

Count your blessings. Muriel's remark continues to exercise me; it's surprising how often I find myself repeating it. It's just a platitude, I know, yet it has come to have significance for me: it seems now less a shallow comment than a deep repository of wisdom to which in the past I have not attended.

It's so easy not to attend to things that are around us all the time. For years I didn't really look at the objects around me in this room: the flowers in the window box, the picture on the wall, the Blue Vase. But now that I do attend to them, they have become full of meaning, beauty and wisdom; they have begun to glow with life, emerging vibrant from their surroundings, their freshness unimpaired by the years of neglect. So it is with a platitude.

Count your blessings!

I feel a desire to flow through life on a sea of platitudes: they are the broad currents, we are flecks of foam thrown up to the surface. We fizz and froth about, too busy to notice the silent current that directs us.

Day 150

A joint visit from Ira and Lachryma today. I had heard nothing of them since the day Ira had snapped at me on the telephone. But today they both appeared after lunch, tiptoeing into my room and talking in whispers.

"We don't want to disturb you," Ira hissed. "We just came to see how you were."

"You've been very quiet," Lachryma said in a barely audible voice. "Are you all right?"

"Fine," I replied. As I spoke, I realised that I was practically yelling the word.

Ira and Lachryma clutched one another, staring at me apprehensively.

"Look," I said more quietly, "please sit down. I'm ... as well as can be expected. So please, do stop whispering."

They sat down obediently. Ira was frowning and Lachryma looked gloomy. They kept darting glances at me as if wondering whether to say something. Finally, Ira cleared her throat and said:

"I'm sorry I shouted at you on the phone the other day."

Even when she was apologising, she sounded truculent.

"That's all right," I said. "I'm sorry if I disturbed you. I just don't know what came over me. I ..."

"That's all right," Lachryma said quickly. "No need to explain. We know what it's like ... losing control."

"Was I making an awful lot of noise?" I asked.

"Frightful," Ira said, nodding.

"Horrifying," Lachryma added in measured tones.

"Oh dear." I felt shocked. "Look, I really am sorry. It's just not like me."

"No," said Ira. "It's like us."

As she spoke, she gave a little laugh – the first laugh I had ever heard from her. And Lachryma's mouth turned slightly upwards in what could have been a smile.

For the first time at that moment I felt some affinity with them. A sense of having made contact, of having shared an experience. I looked at them almost with affection. Perhaps they weren't so bad really.

We remained thus for some time in silence. Then Lachryma said conversationally:

"One of the girls downstairs was asking after you."

"Oh," I said, surprised. "Which one was that?"

"Pavida," Ira said. "We don't ever see the other one."

"And we hardly ever see Pavida," Lachryma added.

"Anyway," Ira continued, "Pavida just asked how you were."

"Oh," I said, gratified. I had no contact at all with the basement-dwellers but it was nice to know that one of them had asked after me.

"Are they sisters?" I asked.

"Cousins," Ira said. "Funny couple, very quiet. We never hear a squeak out of them."

"Yes," said Lachryma. "I was surprised when Pavida asked about you. Usually she never speaks unless spoken to. She generally scuttles past you without a word."

I was reflecting on the contrasting character of my neighbours when the telephone rang. I picked up the receiver and said hello, but the line seemed dead. I put the receiver down again.

"I think someone's trying to get through," I told my two visitors.

"Well, we'll be off then," Ira said peremptorily. Lachryma pulled a long face.

"Call us if you need anything," she said.

And they clattered off downstairs.

I watched the phone for a while expecting it to ring again, but it stayed obstinately silent.

Day 151

No visitors today. I've been talking to myself all afternoon. One result is that I've started wondering who this 'I' is who is talking; and who exactly she is talking to. My thoughts don't seem to be located very specifically in 'me' – rather they seem free-floating; anybody could be having them.

Day 152

I keep thinking about discontinuity, about the way our world is organised in words and objects. What reality do they correspond to? In particular I've been thinking about my body: is it an object? Sometimes it just seems to be an idea in my mind, to have no physical extension at all; at other times, though, when it becomes more physically present, it seems to have no boundary, to be everywhere. It becomes permeable, part of an energy field extending to the ends of the universe. At the moment, though, the energy which should be flowing through me seems dammed up.

I feel that, in a curious way, the weaker I am, the more energy I have trapped within me. It's like constantly ingesting food and never evacuating it. The source of life turns to poison and destruction when it becomes imprisoned. Like life itself. Someone said that destructiveness is unlived life. Illness is unused energy, life turned against itself.

But then again our bodies are not just energy fields: they are storehouses of individual experiences and memories; we each carry a world within us, a unique patterning of the energy flow.

Can we transmit these patterns to our surroundings, I wonder? When we suffer, does the room we inhabit suffer too in some way? Does the atmosphere become heavy? Do the flowers droop slightly and the colours become muted? Conversely, does the room cheer up when we do, becoming light and bright, twinkling at us?

Day 153

Yesterday I wrote about being physically permeable, being co-extensive with the universe. A sort of vanity, perhaps – yet now, I'm starting to experience the same thing temporally.

It happens usually when I'm reading, when I chance on some odd piece of information. For example:

'The younger brother of John Donne was imprisoned for hiding a priest, and died in Newgate.'

Or:

'Margaret Turner was burned as a witch in 1694, having confessed her guilt under torture.'

Or again:

'By God's grace, the woman was suddenly cured of blindness after forty years with this affliction.'

In the past, when I read such things, I was clear that they happened to other people at other times in other worlds; but now, when I read them, I feel they are happening to me.

I languish in prison with the younger brother, regretting perhaps that I'd agreed to take the priest in. But what could I do? There was pressure from my co-religionists. I had to show myself staunch and loyal …

And Margaret, I feel, is not bitter so much as confused. With so many officers of State and Church telling her she is the handmaid of Satan, she has come to believe it herself. How else could she stand the torture …

And suddenly to recover my sight? To look on the

shapes and colours of the world, though at first perhaps I don't clearly see them. How could this miracle have happened to me?

Really, this feeling of everyone and everything being present is quite burdensome. Not only do I have to 'process' my own life's experiences, but now I have to process everyone else's as well. The boundaries dissolve. All experience crowds into the moment.

Day 156

Muriel came this morning. There was a bounce in her walk, and her smile suggested she was savouring ineffable satisfactions.

"Morning," she said, "How are we today?"

"I don't know, Muriel," I said. "Just recently I've been feeling as if I'm disappearing."

"Disappearing! I don't think so, love. If anything, you've put on weight this last few weeks."

I contemplated my body. It was true – I was getting quite bulky. I felt massive and inert, a dead hulk of flesh, a beached whale. If I stuck a pin in myself I'd go phut, phut, phut, and crumple up like a burst balloon.

Muriel, covertly observing my gloomy appraisal of myself, said:

"Don't worry, love. A bit of fat doesn't do any harm. Better than being skin and bone. Now, my Derek – he likes me a bit on the plump side – says it's something to hold on to."

Recently Muriel has got into the habit of making suggestive references to her loved one. Derek, I have learned, is partial to a cuddle, has no reason to be ashamed of his manhood, and likes something a bit out of the ordinary now and then.

Would he like a beached whale, I wonder?

Day 159

A postcard from Eileen today – from Paris!

'Dear Emily, Have run off to Paris for a few weeks with Jean-Claude. Lovely quiet pension, excellent food, indifferent weather – but we don't go out much! All is heavenly – hope things aren't hellish with you.

Thinking of you …

Love, Eileen.'

Everyone else, it seems, has a sex life. I feel envious of Eileen enjoying Paris with her lover – though I can hardly relate to her idyll, because things are hellish with me. I just lie here all day, too weak to stand, too muddled to think, too ill to care.

The odd thing is that other people see me as strong, almost heroic. Any visitors I have from the Social Services or Community Health exclaim in admiration over my fortitude, my patience, my fighting spirit. They encourage me to hang on and have hope; they are certain I'll pull through.

I feel almost an obligation to be the person they see. But that's not the way I feel at all. I feel helpless, desperate and despairing, trapped in an endless nightmare. I feel paralysed, impotent and defeated, unable to rise above my situation. I long for my visitors to recognise my anguish and despair, to remark on it. I do not want to be cast as a hero.

Day 160

A big surprise today: a note under the door from the neighbours in the basement:

'We are sorry to hear you have been ill. We were wondering if you feel well enough to come down for a cup of tea on Sunday at 4?

Look forward to seeing you.

Pavida and Pudora Smith

Basement flat.'

I've been confined to quarters for so many months now that the thought of going out, even as far as the basement flat, seems daunting. And – assuming that I accept the invitation – I shall have to go out at least for a few steps, because the basement flat has a separate entrance. What's more, I shall be entering unknown territory, as I have never in the past been tempted to venture down there. The general atmosphere of wilderness and neglect, combined with the reclusiveness of the two women in the basement, has given the place a rebarbative feel.

I think, though, that I will accept the invitation. It will make a change to go out for tea and I have hopes that Pudora and Pavida will be relaxing company. I can't imagine them displaying the sort of alarming personalities and unpredictable behaviours that characterise my closer neighbours. With a bit of luck, I'll be able to talk to them sensibly, and perhaps discuss doing something about the garden.

Day 162

I have been lying quietly this morning watching God flitting in and out of the clouds. What I've noticed is that His expression never seems to change. Perhaps that's what makes Him so difficult to relate to: he never seems to get upset, gazing upon His suffering creation. He represents Love, Wisdom and Truth, but isn't He ignoring the frequent occurrence in this world of Hate, Foolishness and Mendacity?

I feel more drawn to the pagan gods of the ancient Greeks: they represent the Is of human life, not the If Only. Apollo, for example, is the god of healing and sickness; Demeter presides over both good and bad harvests; Hermes is the patron of both thieves and householders.

They don't particularly care about us, I suppose, the Olympians, but they are like us, readily identified with; they are good for all moods and occasions. Not so the God in my picture: while he concerns himself with Goodness and Light, we are left on our own to find murky and dubious repositories for the darker sides of our nature …

Day 168

I am feeling nervous about my Sunday tea date, nervous about going downstairs. I am so weak that just walking across the room seems like climbing a mountain. Most of the time I just crawl about the flat. But I shall have to do better than that on Sunday.

It's strange to feel so removed from my body. I am quite disconnected from it; I cannot influence it in any way. I feel I'm living with an alien and unpredictable being that is completely oblivious of me. So often when I have an activity in mind, such as 'go to the kitchen and make a cup of tea', I find my body just lying on the couch as if it hadn't heard me.

I live increasingly in my imagination: I picture myself making pots of tea, cutting the lawn, travelling to Paris – and I'm beginning to enjoy the thought of doing these things almost as much as I might actually enjoy doing them – perhaps more.

But that doesn't alter the fact that my body isn't with me. While my fantasy ranges freely, my body persists in its static existence. I long to find some way to quicken it into life. I wept this evening, feeling that I was attending a corpse.

Day 170

Today I made my visit to Pavida and Pudora Smith.

Dear Diary, how shall I give an account of it? I think it will be best if I just start at the beginning and go on to the end.

It was an effort to get downstairs, but I gave myself plenty of time and reached the basement door at 4 pm precisely. (I do pride myself on punctuality.) However, when I rang the doorbell, there was no response. I rang again several times and was beginning to wonder if I had the time wrong when I heard a tremulous voice inside the flat call out:

"Hello."

"Hello," I called back. "It's Emily. I've come for tea – it was today you said, wasn't it?"

After a short silence, the voice replied in a slightly firmer tone:

"Oh, yes, just one moment, please – I won't keep you."

There followed a series of shuffling noises and bangs, accompanied by a whispered conversation. Eventually silence fell and, after a few moments, the door was opened.

I found myself face to face with a tall, thinnish woman, with large eyes and short hair that stood up on end all round her head. Face to face, yes, but not eye to eye. As I held out my hand to greet her, she shrank back and her glance darted from side to side and up and down.

"Oh, please come in," she said to my shoes, and then, "I'm Pavida," she told my right shoulder.

"Pleased to meet you," I rejoined. "I've wanted to for a long time."

This innocent remark seemed to occasion terror in Pavida. Her eyes widened and her gaze became fixed on my left knee. We remained standing thus for a long time in silence.

"Is Pudora with you?" I asked at last, in an attempt to begin a social exchange.

Pavida unfroze.

"Oh, yes," she said, "of course. She's in the lounge. Please come this way."

She led the way to a double door, and then paused as if doubtful about opening it.

"Of course," she said, staring at the door handle, "you know Pudora is very shy. She wants to meet you very much, but – well – you might find her a bit … elusive on your first visit."

She did then open the door and motioned me to enter the room. I went forward tentatively, looking round for Pudora, but the room appeared to be unoccupied.

Tea things were set out neatly on a low table by the fireplace. The table was flanked by two easy chairs, and Pavida gestured me towards one of these. She sat down herself in the other one, nervously eyeing my right foot.

An awkward silence ensued during which I noted that three cups had been put out. This suggested that Pudora would be joining us for tea, though no chair had been placed for her.

"How do you take your tea?" Pavida eventually enquired.

"Just a drop of milk, please."

Pavida poured a little milk into each of the three cups. I noticed her hand was shaking slightly.

"I'll wait a moment for the tea to brew," she said.

Another awkward silence followed.

"Is Pudora not joining us?" I asked presently.

"Oh, she's with us," Pavida said hastily.

She gestured towards a corner of the room. I looked round startled. Surely I hadn't missed seeing Pudora. But there was no sign of her.

At that moment, however, there was a sound of her: a small cough which appeared to come from behind a large tapestry screen placed athwart a corner of the room.

I felt nonplussed. Pudora, it seemed, was behind the screen. Why? Would it transgress tea-time etiquette to enquire? Or should I just accept this arrangement as natural?

I decided I would ask, and turned determinedly towards Pavida, but she was staring in a terrorised way at the teapot, and somehow the words stuck in my throat. I felt altogether paralysed. It seemed as if we would all be there indefinitely: me and Pavida by the tea-table and Pudora behind the screen. Nothing would be done and nothing would be said. A baffling tableau.

Fortunately, however, Pavida made a move: she began to pour the tea. She filled all three cups, and handed me mine. Then she took her own and began to sip from it. Pudora's cup remained on the table. There was no further intimation of life from behind the screen and Pavida and I sipped our tea in silence.

A feeling of resentment, almost of defiance, rose within me. This was a ludicrous way to behave towards a guest – unacceptable. I needed to assert myself in some way, to smash the tableau.

I said rather brusquely:

"Shall I pass Pudora her tea?"

A sharp intake of breath was heard from behind the screen.

"I'll do it," Pavida said quickly. She hesitated and then added: "She was hoping to come out and meet you, but – well – she does find it difficult to face people. Perhaps another time when we've got to know each other better."

She picked up the third cup and went over to the screen with it.

"Pudora," she said, "your tea."

A pinkish hand appeared from behind the screen to take the cup and a muffled "Thank you" was heard.

Pavida remained standing by the screen. She seemed undecided what to do next. The faint sound of a cup scraping on a saucer indicated that the tea was being drunk. Pavida gave me an imploring glance – the first time she had looked me in the eye.

"I can't get her to come out," she said. "Will you try?"

"Me?" I said. "What can I do?"

What could I do? If Pudora wanted to spend her life behind a screen, that was her affair. I hadn't asked to meet her; I hadn't asked to meet either of them. And now I was being asked to rescue them from their social inadequacies.

I felt I should be angry. That would be totally justified. But in fact I was suddenly overcome by an intense feeling of sorrow. What pitiable lives they led, the one terrified, the other too embarrassed to be seen. And both of them stuck together down here in this gloomy basement. How rarely must they have entertained a visitor.

It occurred to me at that moment that perhaps they had never entertained a visitor before, that I might in fact be their first visitor. Perhaps they had felt that my plight called for some sort of response from them; perhaps they had been planning and plucking up courage for our meeting for a long time.

This thought affected me deeply. I can even say it shocked me. At that same moment I felt a strange sensation, a feeling of warmth flooding into the core of my being – as if my heart suddenly brimmed over and poured out love. Love for these two hopeless creatures, who despite their hopelessness, had still tried to make some contact.

Overcome, I put down my teacup and burst into tears. (Did all tea parties in this house end in tears?) Oddly enough, I didn't feel embarrassed; in fact, I felt relieved that something real was happening. Because, after the austerities of the conversation, crying seemed a rich and satisfying activity.

Pavida sat staring anxiously at me. Several times she seemed about to speak, but each time she changed her mind. As my sobbing continued, she pulled her chair close to mine and put a hesitant hand on my arm. She made a low sound, a sort of sympathetic murmur. My sobs abated and I sat distractedly, dabbing my eyes with my napkin.

It was then that another sound was heard: the sound of a footfall somewhere behind me. Someone was approaching the back of my chair.

Could it be? I was unable to look round. I was frozen in anticipation.

The sound came again, a little closer, a little louder but still only on the edge of perception. It must be Pudora, it must be!

I still couldn't look round. Perhaps because Pavida had told me that Pudora found it hard to face people. Perhaps because I found it hard to face her. I could only wait in silence.

The footsteps were very close now and I could sense Pudora's presence behind me. For an awful moment I thought she was going to attack me. But then I felt a light touch, a gentle hand on my shoulder, and the hand gave my shoulder a slight squeeze.

O precious touch!

The hand was withdrawn and the sound of footfalls began again, receding now, fading into silence. Pavida was still holding my arm, and we sat thus without speaking for several minutes.

It was difficult to know what conversation could now be appropriate, and I wondered if I should take my leave. But I didn't want to go without some assurance that I would maintain my contact with the two basement-dwellers, a contact that felt so hard-won and so precious. I considered inviting them back to tea, but it seemed doubtful that they would come. For Pudora, at least, it would be too great a step.

Then a solution occurred to me: the garden. That could be our point of contact. I'd been going to discuss it with them anyway.

A glance through the window more than confirmed the impression I had received from my aerial view: the garden was an unsightly tangle.

Pavida's gaze – and her thought – followed mine, and she said hesitantly:

"We were wondering if we could do something with the garden …"

"That sounds a nice idea," I said enthusiastically. "I'd very much like to help you, but I can't do anything strenuous at the moment."

"Do you know anything about gardening?' Pavida asked. "We don't know where to start."

"I know a bit about plants," I said. "I could suggest a few things. But you'd need to start by clearing it completely – it's hopelessly overgrown."

"We'll start next weekend," Pavida said without hesitation.

I noticed that she said 'we'. This seemed to suggest that Pudora might brave the garden at least.

We sat in silence again looking out of the window. But now the silence didn't seem awkward – rather, it felt calm and harmonious, as if three people were breathing in unison.

I would like to have stayed longer in that silence, but a tea invitation has an etiquette to it, and I sensed that it was now time for me to go.

I rose and thanked my hostess, and, after hesitating a moment, said:

"Please give my regards to Pudora."

Pavida gave me an eager nod, and, as she showed me

out, I just caught a fleeting, timid smile.

So ended our tea party; and, as I crawled back upstairs to my flat, I felt a sense of satisfaction at having paid a social visit – and also some excitement at the thought of collaborating with my neighbours on the restoration of the garden.

Day 171

I've been resting today, recovering from my visit to Pudora and Pavida. It didn't tire me exactly, but I do feel drained.

Drained of what, I wonder? Energy? Emotion?

An odd thing is that, although I feel drained, I don't feel empty. I feel like a space, but not an empty one. Perhaps I should say I feel not so much a space but a place, albeit a place that has little definition at present. It is both within me and also between me and other people. For example, it is between me and those two curious women in the basement.

That brief time I spent with them has changed me somehow. Although physically I am back in my usual place – lying on my couch looking at my flowers – at some deeper level I have changed my location, positioned myself differently in the scheme of things.

In a peculiar way, my inner life seems less inner, more like a 'designated' open space rather than an enclosed area. And, if one thinks about it, is it likely anyway that one has some sort of private life that is secret from the rest of the universe? Unique as we are, all our experience is rooted in some common ground.

Perhaps the reason why my space in the past felt empty and alarming was because it had become fenced off from that common ground, and, like a branch cut off from a tree, had become dead. A cruel act of enclosure.

Day 173

I've been thinking a lot about my body today. It's funny how easy it is to ignore it or forget about it. I'm constantly fretting because my body isn't working properly, because it's 'letting me down', yet at the same time I have very little sense of it.

Since the time, so many months ago now, when I found such reassurance in the consciousness of my breathing and heartbeat, I have consigned my body to oblivion, perhaps as a punishment for its not being right. I have exiled it and told it that it can't come back until it's better. So I have been living bodiless.

But now that I've realised my inner world has no boundaries, it seems even more important to have a body. I need to mark off a section of the universe which is Emily Wentworth. Otherwise I'll be a missing person for ever.

Day 177

Today is Saturday, so this morning I went to sit by the window to see if my neighbours would start on the garden, as promised. Two hours passed and there was no movement down below. I was beginning to think that Pavida had reneged on her promise, when she suddenly appeared on the 'lawn' clutching a cup of coffee. She saw me by the window and gave a timid wave. I waved back.

After sipping her coffee for a while, she took some secateurs and began snipping at roses at the far end of the garden. Pudora did not appear.

However, at lunch-time, to my great surprise, Ira and Lachryma entered the garden carrying what looked like a hamper. Evidently Pavida had had some communication with them about the gardening project. Ira cleared a patch of lawn, spread out a rug and placed the hamper on it. Then she went over to speak to Pavida. A long and earnest discussion followed, after which the two of them came to sit with Ira on the rug.

Lachryma, looking gloomy as usual, opened the hamper and pulled out four plastic plates and four plastic mugs. Meanwhile Ira bad-temperedly tried to open a bottle of wine. Pavida unpacked the rest of the hamper's contents. From what I could see, there was chicken and smoked salmon with lemon, salad, bread, apples and grapes.

When all was made ready, there was a pause for further

discussion. The three of them kept glancing towards the house, and I realised that they were waiting for Pudora to join them. Various beckonings and encouraging gestures were made, but Pudora did not appear. After a while, the other three abandoned their efforts and sat down to their picnic.

They seemed to have forgotten about me, which left me rather miffed. They could have offered me Pudora's share after all. But perhaps they thought I was too ill to go down – and perhaps I was. Still, I would have liked to join them.

After their lunch, Pavida went back to pruning the roses while Ira set about cutting the lawn and Lachryma began burning rubbish. None of them spoke during their work, but, at tea-time, the three of them rendezvoused again on the rug. A whispered consultation took place and then Pavida disappeared into the house. She re-appeared a moment later carrying Pudora's screen. She placed this carefully across the end of the rug closest to the house. She then re-joined her companions. Evidently Pudora had agreed to take tea with them as long as she was out of view.

Tea was poured and a piece of cake placed on each of the four plates. One plate and one mug of tea were placed behind the screen. Ira, Pavida and Lachryma then began to eat and to chat. They made no attempt to see whether Pudora had joined them or not.

But I saw her as she came out – a slim, graceful figure

walking slowly and tentatively across the garden, her face hidden by a large, floppy hat.

I suppose I had imagined that there would be something awful about her, so reluctant was she to be seen. Perhaps she was deformed in some way, or hideously ugly. But her figure seemed perfectly normal and there was nothing exceptional in her walk. Perhaps then it was her face that was disfigured.

She stood hesitating behind the screen, and then, quite suddenly, as if aware of my gaze, she turned and looked directly up at my window. At that moment I saw her face clearly: it was not disfigured at all – in fact, it was quite beautiful, oval-shaped with wide appealing eyes and full lips.

Automatically I raised my arm and waved to her, not expecting a response. But, after hesitating for a moment, she raised both her arms towards me and a smile of pleasure illuminated her features.

Another precious moment! The sun bursting forth brilliantly from a vale of cloud! A bird breaking into song after the night's melancholy! The world seemed to blossom suddenly, as some deep wellspring of life that had been too long underground gushed forth in sudden plenitude.

Pudora turned away and seated herself on her portion of the rug behind the screen. Demurely she began to sip the tea that had been poured for her – and I returned to my couch, overjoyed by my sight of her.

Day 178

Yesterday, when Pudora's smile lighted up the day, I felt I might become magically better – but not so: today the shadows have returned. They gather around me, darkening and deepening, draining light and colour from the world, muting sound and beckoning me into a world where only ghosts move: ghosts stretching out their insubstantial arms, pleading for the lives they have left unlived.

Day 200

The telephone rang this morning. I picked up the receiver and, to my surprise, heard Pavida's voice.

"Hello," she said hesitantly. "Pavida here …" She stopped, evidently wondering whether to continue.

"Hello," I said in my most friendly voice. "I've been enjoying your efforts in the garden. And thank you so much for tea the other week. I've been meaning to send you a thank-you note."

"Oh, that's all right," Pavida said. "It was nice to see you. It's just that … well, I'm ringing because …"

Her voice trailed off again.

I said "Mmm?" in the most encouraging tone possible.

There was a sort of gulp at the other end of the phone and then Pavida said:

"I'm really sorry you didn't meet Pudora. She really wanted to get to know you, but … well, as I said, she does find it difficult to face people."

"But, look," I said, "I did meet her. She gave my shoulder a squeeze. That was much more important than any conversation we might have had. I really felt her presence."

"She will be so pleased to hear that," Pavida said. "She so wants to make friends with someone. We both do, but, well, to be honest, we don't really know how to go about it."

"Well," I said, "I'm sure we can be friends. We made a start when you invited me down to tea."

"Yes," Pavida said – and there was conviction in her voice – "yes, that's true."

On an impulse I said: "Is Pudora there with you now? Can I speak to her on the telephone?"

"Oh," Pavida seemed taken aback. "Well, I don't know, she's never done that before."

"Well, will you ask her?" I said. "She won't have to face me that way, but I'll be able to hear her voice. It'll be a contact with her – like feeling her touch."

"Just a moment," Pavida said. "I'll ask her."

There was the sound of the telephone being put down, and then a long pause during which I could hear faint murmurings and the occasional small exclamation.

Then Pavida's voice came back on the line:

"She's here," she said, "Pudora."

I held my breath in order to listen as closely as possible to what Pudora would say. I imagined she would be inarticulate and speak in a whisper. I was therefore astounded to hear a deep, rich voice saying:

"Emily, hello, is that you? This is Pudora here. I'm so sorry I couldn't meet you properly the other day. I hope Pavida has explained."

"Why, yes," I said, "she did. But in fact no explanation is necessary. None at all. It's so good to hear your voice."

"You'll have to forgive me," Pudora said. "I'm not really used to the telephone. I don't know what to say … and yet there's so much I want to say …"

"Oh Pudora," I cried, "Pudora, of course you do. And there's so much I want to tell you. I've thought so much about you and Pavida since our meeting. I do hope we can get together again soon. Now that we've broken the ice, it might be easier."

"Yes," Pudora's tone became doubtful. "Perhaps, soon …"

"There's no hurry about it," I told her hastily. "Just whenever you feel ready. Come up whenever you like. I'm sure to be here."

"All right, then," Pudora said. "I'll let you know about that. Meantime Pavida joins me in hoping you'll soon feel better."

"Thank you," I said.

"Goodbye for now, then," Pudora said, and rang off.

Day 201

Since speaking to Pudora on the telephone yesterday, I have been haunted by the sound of her voice. Such a warm, rich tone, a glorious full contralto; it still resounds within me, quickening my body.

To think that such richness resides in the reclusive Pudora! What a deprivation that she has screened herself from the world. There is so much beauty in her, so much humanity. Why does she hide away? She is not deformed. Quite the opposite. What makes her unable to face the world? As I write these questions, I feel anger rising within me. Who has inflicted so much shame upon her? How has this happened?

I remember the comfort I felt when she squeezed my shoulder, and I long to run downstairs and comfort her. To tell her everything is all right. To tell her she can come out and face the world, that she has nothing to be ashamed of. To tell her of the love I feel for her.

But I can't get down to her. I am in a very poor state, too weak even to sit up, too weak to go on writing.

Day 202

I collapsed with exhaustion yesterday, and then wept for hours in frustration and desperation. Today I am too weak even to cry – though it feels as though somewhere, deep inside me, my soul is crying, soundlessly and inconsolably. Fatigue overwhelms me and I can only write these few words.

Day 208

I don't recall much about the last few days. I know that they were black and nightmarish. I remember only that I called out Pudora's name several times, and that the memory of her voice alone sustained me in the extremity of my suffering.

Day 209

Eileen telephoned today. She and Jean-Claude are back from Paris and staying in London for a couple of days.

"How are you?" she asked.

I searched in my mind for an adequate answer, and finally said: "I'm still here."

"I should hope so," Eileen said. "Look, can we come and see you. Jean-Claude really wants to meet you and we've got lots of photographs to show you."

I felt panic-stricken. In my subfusc world, how could I contemplate socialising with living beings? In any case I felt too weak to talk.

"I'm sorry, Eileen," I said. "I'm quite poorly at the moment. Can we leave it for another time?"

"Oh, all right." Eileen sounded disappointed. "But I'll be up in London again soon to see about some work – so I shall insist on coming to visit you."

"All right, then,' I said, too weak to argue, and Eileen rang off.

Day 210

Eileen's telephone call yesterday, though stressful at the time, had the effect of drawing me upwards from the land of shadows. I feel able to look about me again and to try to appraise my situation.

I dread these plunges into darkness, fearing that one day I shan't emerge again into the light. I so much want to live, yet I feel that I am dying – not from a physical disease, but because there is some fault-line in my soul, dividing me from myself. Whenever I try to move forwards, I stumble into it.

This evening I spoke of all this to the Blue Vase. How gravely it listened! How benignly it shone! I poured out my whole soul to it, and felt comforted. Then, after lying in silence for a while, I put this question to it:

"O Vase, how can I return to the light?"

The blueness of the Vase deepened for a moment, and then softened. On the sighing breath came the reply:

"Seek the darkness

Know it well

Befriend the shades
Break their spell."
Pondering this advice, I fell asleep.

Day 212

A momentous day! Pudora telephoned this morning and asked if she could come up at teatime. Ever since my telephone conversation with her I have been hoping against hope that she would find the confidence to come and visit me. I so long to meet her!

In a way, though, I feel that I already know her quite well. I have felt her touch, heard her voice, seen her smile, and each of these things has had a profound effect on me. I feel strangely close to her, and protective towards her, almost as if … well, as if she was my child.

Of course I don't really know what she's like. Perhaps she doesn't need protecting. Perhaps she's quite happy living with Pavida and not seeing anyone else.

And yet, if that were true, why should she make the effort now to come and visit me? Because it must be an effort for her. Unless she intends to haul her screen upstairs with her, she will have to sit and face me, and, if I am not mistaken, it will be the first time that she has attempted this with anyone other than Pavida.

It struck me earlier that perhaps I could arrange the room in a way which would make our encounter less threatening to her. Visitors usually sit on the chair opposite the couch, looking directly at me, but I felt sure that Pudora would not be comfortable with this.

I decided to try to move the chair round at an angle to the couch, so that it would be half-facing towards the window. In the old days such things were no sooner said than done, but in my present debilitated state it took me about half-an-hour to get off the couch, crawl along the floor and gradually edge the chair round to the angle I wanted.

By the time I had crawled back onto the couch again, I was completely exhausted. Feeling panicky, I thought of telephoning Pudora to cancel her visit, but it was too much effort even to pick up the telephone. So I just lay still and waited, and fortunately, after a few hours rest, I felt recovered.

Pudora came at teatime, as promised. I heard a quiet but firm knock on the door and called out:

"Come in, it's open."

Pudora came in quietly. I didn't realise she had entered the room until I saw her crossing to the chair. She sat down, her gaze turned towards the window. She was just as I remembered her from the garden: tall, well-built and graceful.

"Hello," I said to her, "Thank you so much for coming up."

Pudora smiled and nodded but she kept her gaze averted.

"I'd like to offer you some tea," I said, "but I'm afraid I'm too weak to get up today. Perhaps …"

"I'll make us some," Pudora said eagerly. Her head turned a little more in my direction.

"Oh, thanks," I said. "You'll find everything you need in the kitchen."

Pudora stood up at once and went out into the kitchen, whence there soon came the chink of crockery and the hiss of the electric kettle. While Pudora was occupied with the tea, I fell to wondering what we might converse about. The occasion seemed so significant that I felt I couldn't possibly be satisfied with a chat about the weather or even the state of the garden. I wanted our conversation to be meaningful, perhaps even profound.

It occurred to me then that perhaps I was being ridiculous. Perhaps I was reading too much into this meeting, dramatising it. A very shy person had made the effort to come up and see how I was, and now she was making me a cup of tea. Fine. Very much appreciated. Surely I could enjoy a cup of tea with her without having to speak memorable lines.

But when Pudora came back into the room with the tea things, all my matter-of-factness evaporated. I was again overwhelmed by a sense of the momentousness of the occasion.

Pudora arranged the tea things on the table and poured me out a cup of tea. She poured one for herself and resumed her seat on the chair, her gaze still slightly averted – though her head was inclined towards me as if she was alert to pick up the slightest sound from my direction.

But no sound came. I was still too overwhelmed to speak. I stared helplessly at Pudora, longing to communicate with her. She was sitting quite still, a preoccupied look on her face. I tried to gather my breath into a sound. I placed my lips in a position that normally produced speech and attempted to expel a word. The effort was enormous, and I felt as if I was gathering in all the energy from my surroundings and focusing it deep down in the centre of my being. At last, a sound emerged, a kind of rasping gasp, a shuddering breath escaping from my depleted body.

It was then that Pudora turned to look at me directly, and I saw the tenderness of her gaze.

"Emily," she said, and her deep rich voice vibrated through me.

I heard myself whisper: "Pudora!"

Softly, Pudora stood up and came over to sit by me on the couch.

"Emily," she said again, and her face was lit by her lovely smile. "Emily, it's all right. We can talk."

She reached out and clasped my hands in hers.

"Oh, Pudora!" I cried. "Pudora, thank God you've come. Oh, Pudora, I do love you so."

Day 216

Three days have passed since Pudora's visit, three days in which I have been floating on a calm ocean. A gentle breeze fans my face and above me the sky is a deep azure blue. I am becalmed, and content to be so. I gaze into the sky's depths and my gaze travels to an infinity. My mind roves the horizon and meets no impediment. My limbs take their ease on the cool cushion of the water. O blessed time of peace!

Day 217

My peace has been well and truly shattered today by the telephone. Several people have called: Muriel to say she's not well and can't come this week; Eileen to say she's off to Nice with Jean-Claude (she still wants me to meet him some time); Ira to ask if I need anything; and Pavida to tell me Pudora had really enjoyed meeting me. Also the telephone rang twice this evening, but the caller rang off when I answered. Wrong number, I suppose.

Day 220

I have been trying to get back into my floating mood but I can't recapture it. Every time I try to imagine myself drifting carefree in the ocean, some little turbulence seems to start up. Nagging currents propel me this way and that, and I have to strain to combat them. The sky darkens, shutting in my gaze, and there is a haze over the horizon. I feel myself tugged downwards, and sometimes waves wash over my face, cutting off the light.

Day 228

I float on the Sea of Limbo, sometimes looking upwards into a grey featureless world, sometimes sinking into an impenetrable darkness. I don't move, but I am not still; a current carries me along.

Day 241

The light is almost gone. Blackness above, blackness below. The last grey streak of light on the horizon rapidly darkens.

The end has been reached: the end of light, of water, of movement. The current no longer carries me. I am cast on a black shore. A sheer precipice rises before me, and at its foot caves gape. From their depths come voices: angry, accusing, anguished, supplicating. Terrible voices – how can I answer them?

I lie helpless in darkness and in torment.

Day 252

For days the voices cried out to me, piercing and wounding me. But now, gradually, they are fading away, receding deeper into the dark caves. Sound, like light, is being drained from the world.

Day 268

I have ceased to inhabit the living world. I feel no pain, no distress, no desire, no fear. Nothing touches me; I experience nothing, not even myself. I write these few words to try to stay alive.

Day 305

So many weeks have gone by now in blankness. Occasionally faces appear before me – Muriel, my neighbours, persons unknown – but I can say nothing to them. The stillness is absolute. Not even a ghost moves.

Except that just now and then, somewhere in deep and arcane regions, there comes a low murmuring sound, caught for a few seconds and lost again. Perhaps I imagine it. But, no, I'm sure I do hear it. A low murmur. There is something comforting in it, as if somewhere in the depths of my being something lives.

Day 348

For several weeks now, I've been listening out for the murmur, and I have gradually become familiar with its habits, attuned to the rhythms of this chthonic presence. It always chooses the moments of deepest stillness, and, if I listen too hard, it dies away. I hear it best when I put myself in a kind of reverie.

Where could this murmuring come from? Is it a feature of the erratic plumbing in the lower flats, or the distant hum of traffic carried on the wind, or the sound of my own blood coursing through my veins, loud-seeming in the stillness?

Today, I sought enlightenment from the Blue Vase, which still stands in its usual place by the window, half-lost in purple shadow.

I meditated for a while, and then, addressing the Vase, as I like to do, in a slightly archaic form of speech, I asked:

"O Vase, whence this murmur?"

I waited in the silence until, on a sighing breath, came the response:

"The spring from which you drink is you,
Let life flow deep, let life flow true."

Day 373

Such feeble strength as remained to me is ebbing away. So many months now struggling to survive, to hope, to function in the most basic way – it seems that in the end the struggle has exhausted me. I have no resources left; I am emptied out.

Beyond hope and despair, too weak to move or to think, I can only surrender to what now seems to be my inevitable decline and probable death. For, even if my physical condition does not kill me, I don't think I can endure further the endless solitary days of illness. I shall be driven, even against my wishes, to end it all. This is the worst torment: to find out how much I can endure!

The blackness deepens. It is frightening but also somehow attractive. It is extinction but also peace and an end to suffering. At this moment all I can do is to surrender.

Day 400

For days after my last journal entry, I have done nothing – just lain and waited for oblivion. I have been suspended between life and death, and I have no desire for one rather than the other. I simply feel dispassionate curiosity about which way the scales will tip. I have no means of weighting them one way or the other.

Day 412

This evening I consulted the Blue Vase again. I had remained aware of its presence even in this time of darkness, but in the place where I have been, words have lost all meaning. Tonight, though, I felt some communication might be possible, and so I addressed the Vase, as always, in a formal manner:

"O Vase," I said, "How can I leave this place of darkness?"

Out of the silence came the sighing breath, and I waited for the Vase to reply. But, though the gentle sighing continued, no reply came. I felt perplexed: the Vase was with me, but it had no words.

Then suddenly something was present, something that had been present before: a murmur. Just barely perceptible.

I remembered that I used to hear it sometimes in the past. Now it had come again – faint but unmistakable. Whence it came is a mystery. It seemed to come through me, but not from me, to be in me but not of me.

Images came into my mind: dark deep churnings of the sea, breezes whispering in branches, coals shifting in the fire's depths, primaeval rumblings in a subterranean landscape.

It was deep, that murmur, deep in the heart of things. There was no menace in it, no protest; it was peaceful, restful. I imagined the cosmos lazily stretching, starting to bestir itself, and giving a small groan of pleasure. That awakening was inside me, held tremulous in the murmur, quickening the senses, exciting currents of energy.

The scales tipped.

I spoke aloud to the unseen presence:

"Sweet, wordless voice, music of life, harmony beyond understanding, be heard, I beg you, in the place and time I call my life."

Day 419

The hum doesn't desert me. It is the companion of my nights and days: a vibration in the air, a vibration within me, a presence, a companion, an alive spirit.

I have begun a dialogue with it – or perhaps I should rather say a duet. I find a note that harmonises with the sound I hear, and hum it to myself for hours on end. It feels so satisfying – I would be content to go on humming like this for ever.

Day 435

Today I thought that working on my hum was like tuning a radio: when I manage to place my voice correctly, there suddenly comes a sharpness and a clarity, not just in my voice, but in the whole of my surroundings. Everything comes into focus.

Day 439

I woke this morning to a different hum, a different presence. Sitting up I saw that Muriel was in the room. She was watering my window boxes and humming a little tune to herself.

"Oh, hello," she said. "Feeling a little better, are you?"

I felt confused. Had I been worse? For the moment I couldn't remember when I had last seen Muriel.

Cautiously I said: "A bit better, thank you."

Muriel gave me a doubtful look.

"You've been proper poorly and no mistake," she said. "Couldn't get any sense out of you at all."

"Muriel," I said. "Have you been every week as usual? – I can't remember …"

"You've been out of it, love," Muriel said. "You didn't know me or anyone else. Those women from downstairs kept coming up – they were dreadfully worried about you. We had the doctor round a couple of times, but he said we should just let you rest – you weren't in danger."

Not in danger! Weak as I was, the absurdity of this statement made me laugh out loud.

Muriel stared at me in astonishment.

"Well," she said, "you are feeling better."

Day 441

It seemed odd to see Muriel yesterday – odd because it was so normal. And today everything still seems strangely normal. I've been lying quietly all day, just noticing my surroundings. Everything seems in place, all systems are working: I can hear the hissing of the water heater, the gurgling of the pipes, the faint buzz of the fridge.

This evening my thoughts turned to the Blue Vase. That, too, was still in its place. Throughout the period of darkness it was the only part of my surroundings that seemed to stay with me. Wordless during the last weeks, but present.

I wondered if it would speak to me again, now that I had come out of the darkness. I wasn't sure, though, what I wanted it to say, what question I needed to ask. I felt a contentment in just being where I was. And yet I wanted some acknowledgement that my circumstances had changed.

I meditated on the Vase for a while and, in the silence, a question formed itself:

"O Vase," I said, "How can I speak of the darkness?"

The silence lengthened, and then, very faintly, I heard the sighing breath, and the answer came:

"Speech is silence.
Dark is light.
Breaks the dawn
In darkest night."

I found this answer very satisfying, and have been murmuring it to myself all evening.

Day 450

I have had a visitor today: Pavida. I felt very pleased to see her.

She sat gingerly on the edge of the couch and looked nervously at me (I noticed that she did look at me).

"Muriel said you were a bit better," she said. "So I've come up to bring you some flowers and see if you need anything. We've all been so worried about you."

I could see it cost her some effort to keep her gaze directed towards me, and the expression on her face alternated between fear and concern. I felt touched that she was striving to overcome her natural timidity in order to be of help to me. How hard people have to work sometimes to express their humanity!

"Thank you" I said to her, and I could hear that my voice was choked with emotion. "Thank you so much!"

"Oh, it's nothing," Pavida said, and then, seeing that I was overcome, she gave my arm a squeeze and busied herself arranging the flowers in a vase and making a cup of tea.

I recovered my composure and we sat sipping the tea for a while in silence.

"You know," I said to her after a while, "I seem to

have had some sort of blackout over the last few months. Have I been here all the time?"

"Oh, yes," Pavida said. "You've been here. One of us has been up every day to have a look at you. But …" she hesitated, and then went on: "You've been elsewhere too."

"Do you know where?" I asked.

"Well, I've got some idea," she said. "All of us have some idea, but we couldn't be exact. Anyway, the important thing is: you're back now."

She gave my arm another squeeze.

"I'll let you rest now," she said, and walked softly from the room.

Day 451

I have been reflecting on Pavida's visit, and in particular, on a phrase that she used: "You've been elsewhere."

Where have I been these last few months? I've reportedly been physically prostrate; yet I've journeyed in a strange land.

Was it the inner world that Eileen once suggested I cultivate? Or was it a region beyond my individual boundaries? It was a dark world, sometimes a dead one, yet I haven't died in it, I have emerged alive.

I wonder, too, if I journeyed alone. I recall the desperate moment when even the Blue Vase appeared to have deserted me, and yet there often seemed to be a presence, a wordless presence … waiting.

Day 452

Talking of companions, which I was yesterday, I had some parlance today with God, that is to say, the God I perceive in the clouds of my harbour picture. It's months since I glimpsed Him, but today He has made some fleeting appearances. I couldn't swear to it, but His expression seems softer, more kindly.

Later:

I have been further studying the heavenly cloudscape, and I am sure I can discern some small winged figures standing beside God. They appear to be singing, and, if I listen intently, I can faintly hear the cadence of their music.

Day 458

I have been humming to myself all day and long to break out into song. I have never been able to sing; my throat just seizes up when I try. But now, straining to hear my heavenly choir of angels, I feel I want to join in, I want to make a joyful noise.

Day 460

I decided I would make an attempt at singing this morning. An immediate problem was that I couldn't remember any songs. I could recall tunes and sometimes first lines, but after that my memory petered out. It was very unsatisfactory: I wanted to sing a complete piece.

One tune which kept coming into my mind was an old favourite of my grandparents: Bless This House. But I had forgotten the words. As I kept humming the tune, though, some words gradually collected themselves together and soon I had a complete song:

Bless this house
You gods above.
Fill it full
Of warmth and love.

Bless this house
You gods below.
Draw back from
Its overthrow.

Bless the people
Who dwell here.
Keep them safe
And of good cheer.

Bless this house

You spirits free.
Grant us peace
And harmony.

Satisfied with my text, I sat up on the couch as upright as possible and tried to sing the song through. My first attempt was little more than a whisper, the second one a croak. But I persisted; I concentrated on my breathing and tried to sing from the abdomen. My voice gradually grew in strength and volume, and I could feel sound vibrating through my whole body. By the time I reached my fifth or sixth rendering, I was filling the whole flat with sound.

So immersed was I in my singing that I failed to notice danger signals from my body. I had gone beyond my strength: my heart was throbbing and sweat was pouring off me. I collapsed back on the cushions, gasping for breath.

But I cared little for my condition. All I could think of was the song, and how I longed to go on singing.

Then, as I lay exhausted, I heard the sound of voices below my window. Women's voices, sweetly harmonising, gently swelling. The sound soared upwards, filling the flat, flooding through me. Magical music, a balm for the spirit and the soul.

I rolled off the couch onto the floor, and, summoning up every ounce of remaining strength, crawled to the window, and looked out.

They were down there in the garden, all four of them – Ira and Lachryma and Pavida and Pudora – standing confidently in the middle of the lawn and singing with all their hearts. Singing my song!

Propping myself up against the window, I breathed the words to myself as their voices rose towards me. How long they went on singing I don't know because I must have fallen asleep where I lay. When I woke up, it was dark, and the night was silent, and I just found the strength to crawl back onto the couch.

Day 464

Today, Eileen arrived unexpectedly – though not unannounced. Muriel, who was just leaving, let her in, and, after several minutes of whispered colloquy in the hall, called out to me:

"An Irish lady to see you."

Eileen marched purposefully into the room and put down a pile of bags on the chair.

"I didn't telephone," she said, "because you always say you can't receive visitors. Well, I'm determined to be received."

"I'm glad you've come," I said. "I'm actually feeling quite a lot better."

"Muriel says you've been in a terrible state," Eileen said. "You really shouldn't have cut yourself off."

"It wasn't my choice," I told her, "and anyway you were in Nice. Where's Jean-Claude by the way? Perhaps I could meet him soon."

"He's still in Nice," Eileen said. She was frowning a little, so I didn't enquire further.

"And why are you in London?" I asked her. "Not just to be received here surely."

"Partly," Eileen said. "I have been worried about you, you know. But partly because of work: there's a chance of a big translation job coming up – I have to see my agent."

"Oh, good," I said.

The world of work seemed very remote, and I felt unable to make much of a response.

Eileen was staring at me quizzically.

"I don't know," she said. "You're in your own world here. Look, relax a bit: I'll make us some tea. I've brought some scrumptious cakes."

We settled down to enjoy our tea and Eileen told me all about her escapades in France. Just like old times! My news never matched up to Eileen's.

After an hour or so I was beginning to tire, so Eileen collected up her things and prepared to leave. At that moment the telephone rang.

"I'll get it," she said. She picked up the receiver and said: "Hello, this is Emily Wentworth's phone."

After a few seconds she put the receiver down again.

"They didn't say anything," she said. "Perhaps it was

someone who wanted to speak to you personally."

"Actually, that's happened a few times before," I told her, "when I answered the phone myself."

"Well, perhaps you didn't sound like your usual self," Eileen said. "You often don't when I telephone. Anyway, let's see if we can recognise their number."

She peered at the display screen and then said:

"Oh, number withheld. How strange. I hope you haven't got a nuisance caller."

She collected up her things.

"Let me know if you have any trouble," she said.

Then she gave me a kiss and left.

Day 465

It was so nice to see Eileen yesterday and to chat with her. On the whole we concentrated on her news because I found it difficult to describe what had happened to me since our last meeting. In fact, I've felt so much better recently that it's hard even for me to picture the world of darkness that was for so long my dwelling place.

Seeing Eileen reminded me of the relaxation book she had sent me. The exercises hadn't helped me much – in fact, they had been quite stressful. But remembering the book made me think about the current state of my body. I was feeling better, but was I now relaxed? I tried to be more aware of how my body was feeling, but it was difficult to get any sense of it – it didn't seem very present.

The relaxation book was still lying about under the couch somewhere. I fished it out and, despite my dubiousness about anything it suggested, leafed through it.

My attention was caught by a section called 'Body Visualisation'.

'To get in touch with how your body feels,' I read, 'conjure up a mental image of it and describe what you see.'

I made an attempt at this.

Another failure: no image came to me. My body was a blank. I wonder if I left it behind somewhere on my journey into the darkness?

Day 470

The mysterious telephone calls began again this morning. I was sipping a herbal tea, and looking appreciatively at the improvement wrought in the garden by my neighbours, when the telephone shrilled out.

I thought it was probably Eileen because she often phoned at the weekend. But when I answered there was complete silence, though the line seemed to be still open.

I put the receiver down, but the telephone immediately rang again. I picked up the receiver, feeling apprehensive.

"Hello, who is it?"

At first there was silence again, but then I felt sure I could hear a faint sound of breathing.

I put the receiver down hastily and switched on the answering machine. I was in too fragile a state to cope with harassment.

Again the telephone rang. I listened to see if any message was left, but there was nothing but a kind of sighing sound, followed by what sounded like a gulp.

The machine clicked off, and immediately the telephone rang again. By now I felt thoroughly rattled and not a little annoyed. Bloody nuisance callers!

I snatched up the receiver and yelled: "Go away, pervert. Leave me alone!"

Then I flung down the receiver.

There was profound silence for five minutes. Good, I thought, that's got rid of the sod.

Then the telephone rang again. The answering machine clicked on and a woman's voice, faint but firm, said:

"Emily, that was you, wasn't it? I'm trying to get in touch with you."

There was a long pause as I strained to recognise the voice. It did seem faintly familiar. I had some sense that it belonged to someone I had known a very long time ago. Some childhood friend perhaps? While I hesitated, the machine clicked off again.

Apprehension gave way to curiosity. Who was it, and

why didn't she identify herself? I waited expectantly for the telephone to ring again. But nothing happened. My caller had evidently given up. I felt quite disappointed.

"Oh," I said out loud, "do ring again."

Obediently the telephone shrilled out and I grabbed it.

"Hello," I said, "I'm here … Your voice – I know it. Please, who are you?"

There was a surprised sound at the other end of the line and then I heard Eileen's voice:

"Emily," she said, "it's me. Are you all right?"

Day 474

I felt better after talking to Eileen on the telephone yesterday. It was a contact with the outside world, I almost said the real world, but of course that would suggest that my life here isn't real. It did feel like that for a long time: I was remote from everything – and everyone – around me. But, gradually, imperceptibly, I have come again to be in relation to my surroundings. Both people and objects have an immediacy which gives vibrancy to my life.

I was reflecting on this when the telephone rang.

I snatched up the receiver and said a breathless "Hello".

"Hello," said a voice. It was the mystery voice of the

previous day! "Is that Emily?"

"Yes", I replied, and waited. I had already decided that, if the voice rang again, I wouldn't be hostile or fearful or impatient. I would just wait and listen to what she had to say.

There was a pause with some throat-clearing at the other end of the line. Then the voice said:

"Hello, this is your body speaking."

My body!

"I've been trying to get through to you for some time."

"Get through?! How do you mean? Why, that's preposterous – you're here. I'm in you."

"I wish you were. I know you think about me sometimes and say we'll get in touch, but we never really have any contact."

I felt dismayed. Just when I was beginning to feel my world was returning to some sort of normality, this had to happen: my body telecommunicating.

"Where are you speaking from?" I asked.

"Oh, just close by. We could meet up if you like. I could drop in."

"Oh, for heaven's sake, you're having me on. Look, if this is a joke, it's gone too far."

"It's no joke, no joke at all, I can tell you. Do you think it's a joke being ignored year after year, getting the blame for everything?"

"But I'm not ignoring you. I'm not blaming you for

anything."

"Oh no? So why are you always saying that you were doing fine until I let you down? Why do you keep saying that I have some mysterious illness? Why are you angry with me?"

"Well, I don't know. I ..."

"Admit it, it's always me that's in the wrong, isn't it? All those crazy neighbours of yours – they behave as outrageously as anything, but that's okay, they're forgiven, they're just suffering humans trying to survive. And that damned Blue Vase – that's your inspiration, isn't it? Your spiritual guide? The fount of all the sodding wisdom in the universe ...'

"Look, please ..."

"And then there's your God, of course – he's always good for a philosophical chat. Oh yes, they're all so fascinating, so enriching, but when it comes to me – oh no, that's different, I'm just that lousy bloody body that's got ill, that won't get better – what a crashing bore!"

"Look, please, I'm sorry – I'd no idea you felt like this."

"No, you never have thought about how I feel. But now you know, because I'm telling you. I've been silent for years, feeling our relationship was all wrong, but not wanting to bother you about it. You always seem so busy, I felt I would be intruding. But now – enough! I've had enough. I'm not taking the blame for everything that's happened to you. If you can't find a place for me in your newly-enriched spiritual and psychological universe, I'm leaving you altogether. Decamping. Levanting. Emigrating. Okay?"

The phone went dead. I remained sitting by it, stunned. I don't know how long I stayed there, but eventually I noticed that I was shaking from head to foot. I lay down on the couch.

Day 475

Needless to say, I have been thinking constantly about that devastating phone call from my body. What she said appalled me – and at first I just tried to blank it out. But the more I ponder it, the more I see that everything she said is true. I have neglected her and I do blame her for my illness. As if somehow she wasn't me. What stupidity! What was I, after all, if not my body? Why, if I was just Mind or Spirit, I wouldn't be Emily Wentworth, I'd just be part of the Universal Essence.

Yes, my body is me, not just a spare part that has gone wrong. I recalled again today that, when I first developed this condition and felt I was losing reality, the first thing that came to my mind was that at least my body was there. I had felt my heartbeat and my breath, and they had reassured me. But, at the same time, they had seemed almost disembodied: the throb and sigh of the Universe. I felt now with conviction that I must embody them.

But how? Where could I find my body? Would she call again? I prayed that she would; suddenly my life depended on it.

Day 480

I have been sitting by the telephone all week hoping that my body would ring. But there has been no call from her. Today I tried to distract myself by watching the activity in the garden below. And there has been a lot of activity. Lachryma and Ira came out at lunch-time and began weeding and generally tidying up. After an hour or so, they were joined by Pavida, who began to snip away at the edges of the lawn.

Watching the three of them so purposefully occupied, I fell to wondering about Pudora. Would she come out? Would she perhaps join the others again for tea behind her screen?

To my pleasant surprise, Pudora came out into the garden well before tea-time. She was wearing her large hat, and I saw that today she had attached a veil to it so that her face was covered. She walked slowly and gracefully to the far end of the garden and began pruning roses.

I stayed by the window watching, and occasionally one or other of the gardeners would glance up and give me a wave. I was struck by their quietness and concentration. They rarely spoke, and each one seemed absorbed in her task; yet there was an almost palpable sense of common endeavour. Every so often one of them would stop her work and stand back surveying the whole garden and give a little nod of satisfaction.

I would have loved to join them, but I knew I was still very frail. Five minutes of weeding and my body would collapse. It occurred to me, though, that there was something I could do.

I waited until four o'clock, and then opened the window.

"Do you want some tea?" I called down to them. "I'll make it."

A chorus of assent floated up. Pleased to be making some contribution, I switched on the kettle and began to hunt for cups and saucers.

It was a long time since I had entertained so many visitors, and it took me some while to assemble a respectable set of tea things. The various items I found didn't exactly match, but neither did they clash, so I felt I was putting on a reasonable show.

Just as the kettle began to boil, there was a small commotion on the stairs, followed by a knock on the door. The guests had arrived!

I opened the door and they made their entrance, each in her own way. Ira banged around a bit, Lachryma stared gloomily about, while Pavida and Pudora, looking apprehensive, came in with linked arms.

I showed them into the lounge and left them to settle while I finished preparing the tea. At first, they sat in silence and I began to worry that the tea-party would be a flop. Soon, however, a low hum of conversation started up. When I went into the room with the tea things, I saw that some fresh flowers had appeared on the table.

"Oh, lovely!" I exclaimed with genuine delight.

Pavida took a deep breath and said:

"We thought you needed something to cheer you up."

Pudora took an even deeper breath. Keeping her gaze fixed steadily on my face, she said: "Are you feeling any better?"

"Why, yes, thanks," I said. "I think I have been feeling a bit better lately – more normal – but I still can't walk much."

"I hope you'll be able to give your lecture in September," Lachryma said in her lugubrious way.

"Lecture?" I said, surprised. "What lecture?"

Ira shifted impatiently.

"Why, the one that's being advertised at the Literary Society," she said. "We've seen the notices for it and we all want to come."

"If that's all right, of course," Pavida added anxiously.

All four of them sat looking expectantly at me.

To hide my confusion, I began to pour the tea and

hand round the cups and plates. This diverted them for a moment and small conversations started up as they handed round cakes to each other. But once they had settled down with their teacups, the expectant silenced was resumed.

"Well, er, what date was the lecture?" I asked, playing for time. "You know, this illness – my memory is a bit affected."

"September 15th', Pavida said promptly. "At 7pm."

"Preceded by drinks and a light buffet at 6.30 in the Byron Room," Pudora added.

"And coffee will be served afterwards in the Upper Gallery," Lachryma said triumphantly.

I took a sip of tea. Unreality loomed.

"Have you written your talk yet?" Ira asked.

"Er … no, not yet," I said.

"Well, I'm really looking forward to it," Lachryma said. "It's got a fascinating title."

"Deep," agreed Pudora.

"Intriguing," Pavida added.

I wondered whether to ask them what the title of the lecture was, but I felt that they might find this disappointing. I made a mental note to contact the Literary Society and find out.

September was still several months away, so there was time to prepare; and presumably the topic was one I knew something about. But would I be well enough to go and deliver a lecture? I had been housebound now for over a year – how could I suddenly appear in a public place?

Still, I felt that, whatever happened, I mustn't let my neighbours down over this; they had expressed such a touching faith in me. I decided then and there that I would start my preparations by going on a small practice outing: as soon as I felt able, I would summon a taxi and go in person to the Literary Society to discover what I was lecturing on.

To my relief, the conversation veered away from the subject of my lecture and focused on plans for the garden. My four neighbours sat for another hour drinking tea and talking enthusiastically of weeding, planting and pruning.

All in all, I felt that the tea-party went off quite well. Ira banged her cup down once or twice, and Lachryma got a bit sulky when someone ate her favourite cake, but they were both quite restrained. And Pudora and Pavida both made great efforts with conversation. Really, they were becoming quite socially skilled.

Before leaving, they all crowded into the kitchen to wash up the tea things, and then, with many expressions of thanks and good wishes for my health, they clattered off downstairs.

Day 500

I have been giving thought to my planned excursion. It seems a big step to leave the security of my home and venture into the outside world – I'm not sure how I shall relate to it. I know that it has been going on its way, 'regardless', as they say, while I have been in captivity. Children in the street not even born when my malaise began are now veterans of the play group. Some people have left the world: the old lady next door and the little girl from the house at the top of the street, the former accompanied by a single car with two mourners, the latter by a long cortège headed by a carriage with black horses.

How will I die, I wonder? How shall I be carried to my final resting place? Not with pomp and circumstance, I shouldn't think. Probably I'll die as I have lived, quietly with a few friends in attendance.

Odd that my thoughts should turn to death just at this moment when I'm about to rejoin the world. Perhaps because over the past months my condition has been a sort of death, and, when close to death, one sees one's life, as if focused under a microscope. One sees it with a rare clarity.

Perhaps the question should be not how shall I find the world to which I am returning, but who is doing the returning? What sort of negotiation can I make with life now?

Day 525

Muriel has been in today. There was something different about her. She seemed more collected, less voluptuously spilling out of her clothes at all possible points. More decorous.

She went about her work in a reflective manner, emitting a little humming sound. When she made the tea, she sat down by the couch and said to me:

"I won't be doing for you much longer."

"Oh – why?" I asked. "Is anything wrong?"

"Oh no, love," she said lightly. "Just the opposite, I'd say. I'm in the family way – just gone three months. I didn't want to say until I was sure things were going okay."

"Oh," I said, feeling nonplussed. "Derek?"

Muriel nodded.

"Congratulations!" I said.

Muriel smiled gnomically. "I'll have to marry him now," she said.

She resumed her dusting and humming.

After she left, I felt outraged. Here was I still barely able to lift an arm and other people were cavorting in bed and having babies. Muriel's activity in life, as far as I was concerned, was hoovering and dusting. The sexual life she had with Derek, though often alluded to, had never had any reality for me; it was beyond the reach of my imagination.

But now it was real, this dark coupling – two months

real. Life does go on; squeezed almost out of existence at one point, it springs up in another as bold as ever.

Day 535

I thought a lot about Muriel's baby today, and felt that in many respects our lives were similar: we were both in a limbo world, a world of darkness, waiting to emerge into the light – and we were both dependent on Muriel!

Day 545

I was sitting around this morning, wondering whether I felt well enough to take a taxi into town, when the telephone rang. I picked up the receiver and instantly recognised the voice on the other end: my body!

"Oh, hello," I said, feeling a wave of relief. "I thought you might not call again."

"Well, I wasn't sure you'd want me to," my body said a little uncertainly. "I was a bit – well – candid last time. So many years of bottling things up, you know, everything just came pouring out."

"Of course, of course," I said. "I understand – you were quite justified. I've thought a lot about what you were saying. I feel very guilty about it."

"Oh, please, there's no need. These things happen,

you know – people just drift apart."

"Yes," I said, "I know, but the awful thing is – I don't remember a time when we were together. I just don't recall you being with me. Why, I doubt if I'd recognise you if I met you in the street."

"I don't suppose you would," my body said. "You were very young when we became separated. We've both changed, I expect."

"Look," I said, "I've got a suggestion. Why don't we get together, meet up for tea or something. Now that we've got back in touch, I don't want to lose contact again."

"All right," my body agreed. "Where do you suggest? Your place or mine?"

"How about meeting somewhere neutral the first time?" I suggested. "I've been housebound for a long time but just recently I've been thinking of making a little sortie into the outside world, to the Literary Society actually."

There was a short pause. Then my body said:

"Oh yes, I know it. There's a little cafe just opposite. We could meet there."

"All right. When?"

"How about Sunday at four?"

"Fine, I'll be there."

"Good."

The telephone went dead, and I sat beside it for a long time, motionless.

Day 548

I spend my time waiting for Sunday; it is still two days away. I feel nervous about returning to the world, and this evening I sought help from the Blue Vase. It still stands in its place on the table by the window, slightly in shadow in the evening. I meditated upon it for a while and then asked:

"O Vase, O Wise One, what does the future hold?"

In the long silence that followed, I began to fear that again there would be no answer. I felt a swirl of confused emotions. But these subsided and I entered a state of peace.

The reply came:

"From the darkness
where the soul weeps
disconsolate;
from the vastness
where the spirit wanders
anguished;
from the deepness
where life murmurs
ceaselessly
flows forth the healing spring."

Encouraged by these words, I spent the evening in meditation and retired early to bed.

Day 550

Sunday at last!

This morning I realised that I needed to confront my wardrobe. For so long now I had slopped about in nightdresses, dressing-gowns and housecoats that I had quite forgotten what it was like to wear ordinary clothes. And, as I had put on weight during my period of inactivity, I might not find anything to fit me.

My survey of the wardrobe was dispiriting. Moths had been at most of the woollens. No two stockings seemed to match, and all the shoes needed attention. Eventually I managed to assemble an outfit that I hoped would not totally embarrass my body: a skirt with an elasticated waist, a smocky blouse, an Anita Brookner cardigan, a pair of tights laddered only at the top, and a pair of slightly scuffed shoes. I felt like a bag lady going on a blind date.

I had ordered the taxi for three-thirty, and by three o'clock, I was all ready and waiting to go and feeling very nervous. I sat by the window for a while rehearsing possible conversations with my body. I supposed that we would exchange news about our lives; I wondered if we had any tastes, interests, or even friends, in common. It would be ghastly if, after all the anticipation of this meeting, we found nothing to say to one another.

Another worrying thought: suppose my body made a scene in the cafe, started shouting, as she had done on the telephone? Suppose she physically attacked me?

I felt myself sweating with anxiety and my heart began to thump. Perhaps I should have a drink to steady my nerves. It was years now since I had drunk alcohol, but I knew there was an unopened bottle of sherry in the kitchen cupboard.

I found the bottle and poured myself a reviving glass. Sitting down by the window again, I saw that there was movement in the garden. My four neighbours had appeared and were gathered in a knot in the middle of the lawn evidently discussing what needed to be done.

They looked up at me and waved.

On a sudden impulse, I decided to go down to the garden and wait for the taxi there. It was a pleasantly warm day, and not only would the company of my neighbours distract me from my worries, but I would be stationing myself halfway to the outside world. To walk from the garden to the taxi would seem an easy transition.

I picked up my bag, smoothed my skirt and went downstairs.

In the garden all was industry. Ira and Lachryma were hedge-cutting. Pudora was sweeping the shorn branches into piles, and Pavida was heaping them into black bags. They all worked quietly with great concentration, stopping occasionally to smile or nod at me.

I sat in the middle of the lawn, marvelling at the transformation of the garden from tangled wilderness to delightful arbour. I was pleased they had not made the place too neat and orderly: there were no regimented flower beds, just a natural arrangement of plants, shrubs and flowers. The colours were enchanting, the scents alluring.

I was roused from my contemplation of this beauty by murmurings and movement close by me. The four gardeners had paused in their labours and had come to sit beside me.

"It's good to see you down here," Pavida said.

"We thought you'd never come down to see our efforts," Pudora added.

I always felt very appreciative when they took the initiative in conversation because I knew how hard this was for them.

"It's marvellous," I told them. "I only wish I could have helped."

"But you did," Ira said.

"You got us started," Lachryma concurred.

Even now I thought, the one sounded a bit snappy and the other a bit doleful, but, compared to how they used to be when I first met them, they were practically normal.

I decided to confide in them about my outing.

"Look," I said, "I'm feeling a bit nervous. I'm going out – on a sort of blind date."

"A date?" chorused four surprised voices.

"Yes, well, not a date exactly, more a reunion. A friend, that is to say, my body, has started telephoning recently and I'm going to meet her for a coffee."

"Your body?" said Ira, sounding rather impatient. "Well, that's perplexing. Your body is here now – how can you be meeting it?"

"It's hard to explain," I said. "Of course, it's always been with me in a way, but, well – it's like a stranger."

"Oh, I see," said Lachryma doubtfully. "Well, I hope you get on with it."

"You're very brave," Pavida said. "I'd never have the courage to meet someone like that."

"No," said Pudora, "it would be so embarrassing in a public place."

"Look," I said, feeling exasperated. "I was hoping you'd give me a bit of encouragement. It's the first time I've been out for ages, you know, and the first time I've ever been on a blind date."

They all looked contrite.

"Would you like me to take you on the scooter?" Ira asked. (She was the possessor of a small motor scooter which she used mainly for shopping.)

"It's okay, thanks," I said, mollified. "I've got a taxi coming."

I did feel quite tempted by Ira's offer. It would be reassuring to go to this meeting with a friend, but two things deterred me: one was that, if I went on the bike, I would arrive in sartorial disarray with my hair mussed up; and the second was that I had a secret part of my mission to fulfil: to go to the Literary Society and find out what lecture I was giving in September.

My four neighbours were now murmuring anxiously together and giving me sidelong looks.

"At least come and have a cup of tea with us when you get back," Lachryma said, "and tell us what happened."

"Yes," said Pudora, who was uncharacteristically giggling. "We can debrief you."

The others burst out laughing at this, and Pudora became self-conscious and blushed.

At that moment, the taxi drew up outside the garden gate. Accompanied by many good wishes and sundry cautions and admonitions, I got into it and waved my neighbours good-bye.

"Where to?" asked the driver.

"Literary Society, please," I said, "Market Square."

It was only a ten-minute drive into the town centre, and to my driver no doubt a routine one.

To me, however, it was a momentous journey. For the first time in nearly two years I was out in the world, gazing like a tourist at hedges, gardens, houses, shops; at people trudging along with shopping bags or pushing prams or running for buses. Yes, it was business as usual in the world: even the winos were still sitting drinking on the park benches. I felt shocked at the sight of rubbish on the streets and the graffiti on the walls. It was all still there, including the misery and the ugliness.

How I had longed in all the housebound years to be out again in the world. But my initial reaction was not elation, more a feeling of flatness and disappointment that the outer life had not transformed itself during my absence.

The traffic was light and we soon reached the Literary Society. Having paid off the driver, I stood uncertainly on the pavement for a few moments, aware that my legs were very weak. The sooner I went and sat in the cafe the better.

But first, my lecture! It was something of a shock to see not only my name but also my photograph on the public notice board outside the Society. I drew closer and read the following:

September 15th
7 pm
Dr Emily Wentworth,
distinguished writer and translator,
will give a talk entitled:
Layers of Meaning

Perplexed, I stared at the notice, and my face stared back at me. My public face! I wondered what impression it made. It was hard for me to judge. It struck me as a serious face, thoughtful, perhaps wistful. As I stared at it, my eyes filled with tears. Not tears of sorrow or pity, just tears of recognition.

At that moment, I felt a light touch on my arm and a familiar voice said:

"Emily? Is it you?"

My body! She was here!

I turned towards her. A wave of emotion overcame me, and, with a choking cry, I threw myself into her arms.

An unusual way to begin an acquaintance. But I didn't care: I just stood in the middle of the street, clinging on to my body and howling my eyes out.

Fortunately, my body seemed equal to the occasion. She hugged me close to her, making sympathetic noises and waving away curious passers-by. When my sobs had abated a little, she gave me a handkerchief to wipe my eyes and blow my nose.

"There, there," she said soothingly. "No need to be upset. Shall we go inside and find a table?"

Still snuffling, I nodded gratefully and followed her into the cafe.

"My usual table's free," my body said.

She led the way to a small table for two in an alcove by the window. It had a pretty tablecloth and a vase of fresh flowers upon it.

"Do you come here often then?" I asked.

Sadness came into her face as she said:

"Yes, I started coming when you began to lecture at the Literary Society. I saw your talks advertised in the paper and … well, it seemed like a way of being close to you."

I digested this remark in silence while the waitress took our order, and then asked:

"But why didn't you attend the talks? Why sit here in the cafe?"

My body hesitated.

"I don't know – I just wasn't sure I'd be welcome."

I felt tears welling up again.

"You mean you've been coming here all these years …" My voice broke.

"Yes. It made a nice outing actually – sort of gave me a point in coming here. I used to see you leave after the lectures – and I felt, well, it's good that one of us is doing something useful."

"But I've been ill,' I said, "for months now. I haven't been giving any lectures."

"I know – I was worried about it at first, worried that perhaps you might have … gone away. Anyway, I kept coming here on Wednesdays, hoping you'd appear. But then I heard some people saying you were very ill and it would be a long time before you could work again. Well, I waited and waited. Weeks and months went by – and in the end I got sort of desperate to get in contact with you. That's why I phoned."

We lapsed into silence again while the waitress laid out the tea things and put a plate of cakes on the table.

My body began to pour out the tea.

"Is it still milk and no sugar?" she asked.

"Yes," I said.

"Cake?"

"Thank you."

We sat in silence for a long time sipping tea and nibbling the cakes.

Finally I said:

"I feel awful – you've gone to so much trouble to find me, to stay in touch. The thought of you sitting here waiting day after day – it's intolerable."

People at nearby tables were giving us curious looks and I realised I was crying again. My body leant over and squeezed my arm.

"It's all right," she said. "It'll be all right, we've found each other now."

"Please," I sobbed, "please – don't try to comfort me, don't tell me it's all right, it's not all right, it's not all right – all these years, all this longing and loneliness, it's not all right."

My voice was becoming shrill. The conversations around us died away and a waitress moved uncertainly towards us.

"It's not all right!" I was shouting now. "These things shouldn't happen." I banged down my cup on the table. "We can't get these years back. It shouldn't happen, it shouldn't happen!"

The people at the next table began to collect their belongings, and the waitress, in company now with the manager, approached determinedly.

My body got up and came close to me.

"Please," she said, "don't! Everything's all right now."

I started throwing things – anything within reach: teapots, teacups, vases, Eccles cakes – they all went flying.

I was yelling – yelling and yelling:

"Sod the bastards who did this! Sod the bastards who separated us! Sod them!"

I felt a strong pair of arms around me and found myself propelled towards the door. Blind with rage I struggled to get free. I heard a voice say:

"It's all right – she's been very ill. Very ill. I'll make good the damage."

"Murderers!" I shrieked. "Violators! Oppressors!"

I thought I was struggling with the manager, but, as I tumbled out onto the pavement, I saw that it was my body who was gripping me.

Drained of strength, I sank to my knees and silently pummelled the paving stones with my fists. My body knelt down beside me, murmuring words of comfort until eventually I became still.

We stayed kneeling in silence for a few moments and then the blackness which had fallen over my eyes receded and my surroundings came into focus.

The first thing I saw was a row of wide-eyed faces ranged in the cafe windows above me. The manager and the waitress were standing in the doorway muttering doubtfully to one another. The scene remained frozen for an endless moment and then my body said:

"Not quite your usual lecture!"

At this we both collapsed in laughter, and, as heads in the cafe windows began to shake, we succeeded in making our escape. I saw a taxi coming down the street towards us and flagged it down. We scrambled into the back seat, clutching each other and giggling.

The taxi driver, regarding us wearily, asked:

"Where to, ladies?"

As I hesitated, my body said hastily:

"Do you want to drop me off first?"

I suddenly realised that I didn't know where she lived.

"Do you live in town?" I asked.

"Yes, in digs, in Central Avenue."

"Oh."

I still hesitated. After all that had happened, I didn't want to just drop her off. In fact I felt strongly that I didn't want to part from her.

"Won't you come back with me and have some tea?" I said. "After all, we didn't really manage to have any in the cafe."

"Would that be all right – I don't want to impose."

"Of course you must come, and you can meet my neighbours. We can have tea together in the garden."

The driver, an expression of resignation on his face, said:

"Decided then?"

"Number two, Church Lane," I told him.

We bowled along at a fair pace and my body and I fell

silent. No obvious conversational topic presented itself and I began to wonder if I had done the right thing in asking her back to tea. I very much wanted to know her better, and to thank her properly for her help, but I felt suddenly constrained.

And then, what about my neighbours? Could they be relied upon to behave properly at tea? They were still so unpredictable – I didn't want my first face-to-face meeting with my body turned into a fiasco.

As the taxi drew up outside our gate, I saw all four of my neighbours sitting in the garden. To my surprise, they appeared to be taking tea in a very formal way. They had changed out of their gardening clothes and were wearing pretty cotton dresses and straw sunhats. They were demurely sipping tea out of china cups. The garden table had been covered with an embroidered cloth and upon this were placed delicate plates bearing tiny squares of cucumber sandwiches and dainty cakes.

I saw my body hesitate, but she got out of the taxi and waited while I paid off the driver.

"I'm just a bit casual," she said.

"It's all right," I told her. "They're not at all stuffy or formal really. They've been gardening like mad all afternoon – I expect they wanted a change."

As we went through the gate, a thought struck me.

"I'm not sure how to introduce you?" I said. "It sounds a bit odd to say: This is my body."

"Yes," my body replied, "I understand. And actually

I'd prefer it if you used my real name, Comita."

"Comita!" I repeated the name a couple of times, and then asked, "Does it mean something?"

"It means companion," she replied briefly.

I waved to my neighbours and called out: "I've brought my friend, Comita, back to tea. Have you got two extra cups?"

Then I saw that two plates and two saucers with upturned cups had already been placed for us on the table.

Day 551

The tea party yesterday went quite well – better than I had expected, to be honest. Comita seemed to fit in all right and, as the tea progressed, my four neighbours gradually dropped their ridiculous pretence of formality and started behaving more naturally. Ira threw a small tantrum over not getting her share of cake, and Lachryma had a little cry into her teacup at one point. The other two were very quiet, communicating mainly in monosyllables. All the same, there was a comfortable sort of atmosphere, a feeling that, despite temperamental differences, we belonged together – like a family.

Eventually my four neighbours said they had to get back to the gardening and Comita and I were left alone.

"You know," I said to her then, "it's funny – I've only

just met you, but you seem so ... well, familiar – as if you've always been here."

"Yes," Comita said, nodding thoughtfully. "It does feel like that. Coming here is just like coming home."

"I wonder," I hesitated a moment. "I wonder – would you like to make this your home?"

"You mean, live here?"

"Yes, with me. There's plenty of room. You could be as independent as you wanted."

"Well, that's tempting," Comita said. "I think I'd like it, but what about you? You might miss having the place to yourself. Perhaps we shouldn't do anything impulsive?"

"Oh, let's be impulsive," I said. "After all, if it doesn't work out, we can always separate again. And anyway, just because we're inhabiting the same space doesn't mean we can't still have some independence."

"That's true," she agreed. After a few moments' reflection she said:

"All right, I'll come then! When would it be convenient for me to move in?"

"Today," I said without hesitation. "We can ask Ira to go and pick up any clothes you need immediately and sort out the rest tomorrow."

And so it was that Comita came to stay.

Day 565

Comita has been in residence for two weeks now. I've had some nervous moments wondering if it was the right decision to invite her to move in, but on the whole I feel confident that the arrangement will be a success.

I suppose that when you live on your own for a long time, you do get a bit selfish, even a bit cranky. At first, I did find it irritating to keep coming across evidence that Comita had been using the bathroom, or to find her sitting in my favourite chair. Frankly, she does tend to sprawl and generally slop about, and I'm used to being quite neat and compact.

Also, she has a characteristic smell which I've had to get used to: not in any way an unpleasant smell, just a smell of a living being around the place. For the first couple of days I was splashing lavender water about to disguise it, but then I thought no, you're being too dainty. There's nothing wrong with a body smell.

She has been quite considerate, I must say. The first few days after the drama of my outing I felt quite fatigued and had to rest a lot. She was very good about making meals and cups of tea. And it's a great reassurance to have someone around at night. The nights are a difficult time, especially when I feel ill, but, with Comita at hand, I have some comfort and security. If I can't sleep, I listen hard until I hear the sound of her breathing, and I let myself float away on her breath. I feel the rhythm of it and I lose myself in it. Until now, I had relied on my flowers to sustain life in the flat when it had flickered out in me, but now I have the breath of a whole body.

Day 575

Muriel came this morning. She had been off ill for a couple of weeks so it was the first time that she had met my new flatmate.

"Well," she said to me as we all sat down for a coffee together, "you're looking a lot better. It's done you good having your friend here."

"Yes," I said. "And I think we'll be making it a permanent arrangement."

Muriel gave a nod of satisfaction.

"That's good," she said, "because I'm going to have to stop work earlier than I thought." She looked at me significantly and added: "Blood pressure."

"I hope it's not serious," Comita said.

"Not yet," said Muriel. "But the doctor says it's best I rest as much as possible."

"Well," Comita said, "Emily will be all right – I can do the housework now and the shopping."

"And soon I'll be able to help a bit, I'm sure," I added.

Muriel nodded. "When the baby's born," she said, "will you come to the christening, Emmy – and your friend too of course?"

"Certainly we will!" I said. "It's a date."

Day 576

After Muriel left yesterday, I felt a little sad. Her departure seemed rather sudden and I was glad I would have the opportunity to see her again. We've never talked a lot together, and I suppose there has been some tacit acknowledgement that we differ in our tastes and interests, but there has always been a mutual liking and respect, a very human contact that didn't depend on words.

It's been helpful, too, to have the outside world looked after so meticulously. Muriel has always been a true professional: no skimping on the cleaning or the polishing; and she always took care to buy and prepare me appetising foods.

For so long there seemed little correspondence between my inner turmoil and the shining neatness of the flat; yet I always felt grateful I didn't see around me the projection of that murky distorted inner world of mine. To feel that somewhere there was order, routine, schedules, attained goals – this was important; there was pleasure in seeing things looking their best, cared for, respected: the table newly polished, the kitchen floor gleaming, the glasses sparkling.

When you feel too empty to love the world, at least you can still appreciate it.

Day 590

Comita and I have been talking about Muriel today.

"She seems a nice sort of person," Comita said.

"Yes," I said, "I'll miss her. I think Derek's a lucky man."

"Derek – is that the husband?" Comita asked.

"Husband-to-be, yes."

"Oh," she seemed to hesitate, and then said: "You used to be married. Your husband was called Jake, I think."

"Yes, do you remember him? When he was killed in the car accident, it turned my life upside down for a long time."

"Has there been anyone else since?" Comita asked.

"I've had one or two relationships but they weren't really satisfactory. What about you?"

Comita looked thoughtful.

"Mixed fortunes," she said. "Passing trade. Not very satisfactory either – but what is a body supposed to do?"

Her face became downcast. Then, brightening, she said:

"The first one, James, you might remember him. You knew him when we used to knock about a bit together at college."

I cast my mind back to try to remember James. I didn't want to say I couldn't remember him because I knew Comita was still very sensitive about my not recalling any of our past life together.

As a diversion, I asked:

"Have you got a boyfriend at the moment?"

"No-one at the moment," she said. "Well, to tell the truth, this last year or so I've been so preoccupied with our relationship, or lack of it, that I haven't thought of much else. Not that I wanted a sexual relationship with you, of course, but I have wanted a physical one. I didn't want to go on just reading your translations and attending your lectures. I wanted some proper contact with you. I couldn't really get interested in anyone else until I'd got my relationship with you sorted out."

"And now?" I asked.

"I don't know," she said. "What about you?"

"Well, I lost my sexual urge when this illness started – and it feels like a sort of liberation. I'm not sure if I want to be bothered with it again."

"But perhaps now you're getting better, you'll feel differently?" Comita suggested.

"All that seems very remote," I told her. "I couldn't even imagine that Muriel was having a sex life – until she got pregnant, and then it suddenly became real. But for myself … well, perhaps if you found someone, then I might start thinking in that direction again."

Just then I remembered about James and we started to reminisce about our college days.

Day 591

My conversation with Comita yesterday has set me thinking. Not about sex specifically, but about life in general. Sex may not be exactly the pinnacle of human achievement, but it does represent some vibrancy of living. It takes energy, and energy is what I've been lacking for so long. Just to be even thinking about sex must mean that some energy is present. I've noticed throughout this recovery period that once the mind is able to conceive of something, it's not long before the body becomes able to do it.

And energy is coming back – I've been able to do so many more things these past few weeks. I've been out, after all, and, well. . . wrecked a cafe. (Comita has been back to the cafe since and arranged compensation – she hinted that I was menopausal and that seemed to satisfy them.)

It wasn't a very auspicious way of returning to the world, but it was an energetic one. Now that I seem to be on the move again after such a long spell of lying becalmed, what direction shall I take, I wonder?

I don't feel I'll be seeking anything; I shan't be on a quest – I'll just wander about exploring. After my recent journey to Hades, I shall be content simply to potter in the upper world.

Day 610

Eileen came to tea today. I had telephoned her to say I was feeling better and wanted to invite her.

She bounced in, ebullient as ever.

"So, how are you?" she said. "You look a lot better."

"I feel so," I said. "How are you?"

"Do you want the good news first or the bad?"

"You choose!"

"Bad news is Jean-Claude and I have split up."

"Oh, I am sorry. I thought that was working out."

"So did I."

"What happened?"

"I don't know – things just changed. I don't know why or how (and there isn't a who, by the way). We just ceased to communicate in any meaningful way. There was no point in us being together anymore."

"You don't seem broken-hearted about it."

"No, just mystified."

"What's the good news?"

"Well, that affects you. I've got a commission for a translation: a history of the Enlightenment in France, three volumes altogether. It's a lot for me to do on my own, and I wondered, as you're feeling better, if you'd like us to work on it together."

"Why, yes," I said, "yes … I think I could manage something – once my lecture's over anyway."

"What lecture is that?" Eileen asked.

I told her about it and she said she wanted to attend.

That means a party of six I'll have with me: my four neighbours, Comita and Eileen. They'd better let me in this time!

Day 611

After Eileen's visit, I felt elated. Elated at the thought of work, of collaborating on a project, of being connected to the world again. I said out loud: "Thank God I'm getting better."

That reminded me that I hadn't seen God for a while. I used to be always conscious of His face in the picture, flitting in and out of the clouds, but recently He had disappeared from view.

It wasn't often I thanked Him for anything – there was so much to blame him for; in fact, hardly a day went by without me having a good Jobian rant. So it was a shame that now, when I was finally ready to give some thanks, I found it hard to discern His image among the clouds. I stared hard at the picture but it remained obstinately a depiction of a lighthouse under a turbulent sky.

I tried a catching-Him-off-guard approach. I avoided looking at the picture for a long time and then darted a sudden glance. But … nothing! He remained invisible. Evidently He had no need of thanks.

Yet I feel I must give thanks to someone, or something, for my recovery. Of course I can, and do, give thanks to my neighbours, Comita and my friends for all they have done to help me. But I know that it is not they who have orchestrated my recovery; thanks for that must go to some unfathomable intelligence, some guardian spirit that accompanied me through this journey back to life – and which no doubt would have accompanied me on my journey to death if the scales had tipped the other way. It's that companionship I want to give thanks for.

Day 619

The Blue Vase seemed very present this evening. It shone out in its deepest blue and sent out sighing breaths across the room.

I lay and meditated upon it, trying to adapt my breath to its rhythm, and soon I became aware of small mist-like wraiths floating up from the Vase and curling round the room. As I watched, one of the wraiths floated above the rest and began to resolve itself into a series of shapes. The shapes came and went, forming and re-forming themselves, until they became recognisable as letters. Then the letters twirled and swirled around the room until they finally came to rest above me in the shape of a familiar word. I said it out loud: "LOGOS".

Not just any word, the Word. The word beloved of the ancient sages, the word that was God. As it hung above me, I felt its full force and majesty, its power and its symmetry. Again and again I pronounced it:

"LO ... GOS, LO ... GOS, LO ... GOS.'

Each time I spoke the word, my breath dissipated the wraith-like forms above me, but, as I drew breath in again, they re-formed themselves as LOGOS.

"LOGOS, LOGOS," I repeated, and "LOGOS, LOGOS," they replied.

Then a second mist-like shape floated towards me, and again letters danced and whirled until another word was formed. Joyfully I pronounced it: KOSMOS, KOSMOS, the harmony of the universe, the rightful order of things.

For a long time I lay whispering these lovely orotund words while the vaporous forms played in the air, turning themselves from letters into coiling ribbons, and then back into letters again. So we continued for an endless time, the words dancing, the Blue Vase sighing, me breathing, all joined in some divine harmony.

Day 624

Things have been going so well generally that it is a little disappointing to record that there is a discordant note. I am referring to relations between my new flatmate, Comita, and my long-term companion, the Blue Vase. I regret to say that the two of them do not seem to be getting along.

Of course I realise that a Blue Vase will not appeal to everyone, and indeed that my relationship with it might seem eccentric. But it has been so very important to me and remains so. I still spend some time with it every evening, sometimes talking to it, sometimes just contemplating it. And, when I do feel in need of an oracle, it is never disobliging. It has a wisdom, a thoughtfulness, a loving presence that I just could not be without any more.

I have tried to explain this to Comita. I suppose that initially I had just assumed that she would like the Blue Vase – our tastes do generally coincide – and find it a source of strength. But she seems, if not hostile, at least ambivalent towards it.

In fact the other day she suggested removing it from its place by the window and putting it on the ledge in the stairwell. I felt dismayed.

"But that's not even in the flat," I said. "That wouldn't do at all."

"Oh, I'm sorry," said Comita. "I know you're attached to it, but I thought, now you're so much better, and I'm here, it wouldn't seem so important to you."

"You don't like it, do you?" I asked her.

She hesitated and then said:

"Oh, I wouldn't say that – I just don't see the point of it. It doesn't even have any flowers in it. You might just as well keep it in a cupboard."

I felt sure I saw the colour of the Blue Vase darken as Comita said this, and I thought I heard a sigh. But a shaft of sunlight caught the Vase at that moment and at once it gleamed out brightly again.

Comita, however, was frowning and silent.

I felt very troubled by this exchange. Two presences that were crucially important to me were not in sympathy with each other. How could I reconcile them and find some way for us all to live together? For live together we must: I had committed myself to sharing my home with Comita, and I had no intention of putting the Blue Vase on the stairs.

"I'm not moving it," I told Comita firmly. "But, if you want, I'll think about putting some flowers in it."

It was the best I could do by way of a compromise.

Day 628

A red-letter day. I have been out shopping.
Eileen came over this morning and drove me into the town centre. Our mission: to buy me a decent outfit to wear for my lecture at the Literary Society.

I was planning to wear my cotton dress with the Greek meander pattern that usually serves on formal occasions, but Eileen, who assigned great importance to the occasion of my lecture, insisted that I get something new.

"And you can have a decent hair-do," she said imperiously. "We've got the contract for the translation, so you can afford to splash out a bit."

All the same, I hadn't intended the splashing-out to extend to buying a designer outfit in expensive silk and what seemed like a whole wardrobeful of accessories.

"Now," Eileen said, when the shopping was done, "to the hair salon."

"Is it really necessary, do you think?" I said feebly. "I think my hair looks all right as it is."

Eileen said firmly: "I've made you an appointment with Raymond at two."

I nodded meekly.

While Raymond was styling my hair, he pointed out that my skin was in poor condition, and immediately Eileen insisted that I should have some beauty treatment as well. I submitted without a fight.

At teatime, my transformation complete, we repaired to the Edwardian elegance of the Criterion Hotel. As we entered the restaurant, I found it hard to recognise myself in the long mirrors that lined the wall. Was this elegant creature really me?

Once we had taken our seats and our order had been brought, I felt more relaxed and even began to savour the occasion. The delicate aroma of Lapsang Souchong, the inviting smell of buttered toast, the delicious cakes, the fineness of the china: how alluring, how civilised! Especially compared with the horror and violence of my previous tea-time outing with Comita. Recalling my apprehension on that occasion, my cobbled-together outfit, my hideous outburst in the teashop, I could only marvel at my present elegance and composure.

Around us a low murmur of voices rose and fell, cups chinked discreetly, and from the far corner of the room came the soft sound of a piano – the music was a Chopin Impromptu.

So – there we were: two fine ladies taking our tea in civilised surroundings. The moment seemed enchanted. A new life beginning. Only this journal will hold the record of the nightmare.

Day 629

After the excitements of yesterday, I have been enjoying a quiet and reflective day. Eileen and Comita, who seem to get on quite well together, have gone for a walk, and so I have had some time to myself.

To myself, but not exactly by myself. For I have with me the two companions who have been by my side constantly throughout the ordeal of the past two years: my journal and the Blue Vase.

And the past two years have been an ordeal, though now, looking back, I can see that many good things have come out of it. Most importantly, I've made friends with my neighbours and welcomed Comita back into my life. Probably I would never have got acquainted with any of them if I hadn't fallen into such a vulnerable state.

Also, I've had time to think a lot, and, in some curious way, I've simplified my life – got rid of a lot of clutter and come to focus on what's really important. What that is, is hard to define: I can only say that part of it is being able to be truly myself, to take up my space confidently in the universe, to be capable of tenderness towards myself and others …

Day 637

I think I shall soon bring this journal to an end. I have decided to go on writing it until the day of my lecture; after that, I shall return to my old-style appointments diary. It's important to be able to end a journey.

Day 639

My room has seemed so peaceful this evening. The house is quiet and outside the night is calm and clear. After sunset, I left the curtains slightly open so that I could watch the Blue Vase shading into the darkening blue of the sky.

Softly I spoke to it:

"O Vase, companion of my nights and days, my oracle and solace, my joy and delight, I venerate and thank you."

I ceased speaking, and from the deep, deep silence that followed there came a faint murmur, a sweetly sighing breath. The blue of the Vase shone radiantly for a moment and then became muted again. Then came the words, the last words that the Blue Vase ever spoke to me:

"Fare well, my friend,
Our way was long.
Yours now the poetry,
Yours the song."

The stillness deepened. I became the stillness.

Day 640

11.00 p.m.

I have done it! I have actually done it! I have been to the Literary Society and delivered my lecture. What a day!

It's late now and I'm tired and I really long to go to bed, but I made a promise to myself to conclude my journal today – and I've got just one hour left to do so.

The day unfolded as follows:

The morning was uneventful. I rose late and spent a long time bathing and dressing and generally grooming myself. I then had a light lunch (which Comita prepared) and studied the notes for my lecture. This being my first professional venture for nearly two years, I wanted to give a competent performance.

When I was satisfied that I had made all the preparations I could, I lay down and rested. Eileen and the neighbours were due for tea at five, and at six-thirty we were all going together to the Literary Society. Two taxis had been ordered.

I must have dozed off because I was suddenly startled by the ringing of the telephone. I felt a foreboding that something had gone wrong, that the lecture had been cancelled, that I had been reported missing again. But, when I picked up the receiver, I was reassured to hear Muriel's voice.

"Hello, Emmy," she said. "How are you?"

"Fine," I said. "How are you?"

"A bit tired. I'm phoning you from the hospital to tell you we've had our baby – a little girl. She came a lot earlier than expected! She's called Daisy."

"Oh – congratulations!" I said. "That's marvellous news! Are you both all right?"

"Derek thinks we are," Muriel said. "He's as pleased as pie."

"I'll come and visit you soon, if I may," I said. "I'm getting out and about a bit now."

"You've got over your Fatigue, then?" Muriel asked.

"I do believe I have," I told her.

We made arrangements to meet, and she rang off.

I sensed that Muriel's call was a good omen, but I still

felt anxious about the evening. However, I was refreshed by my rest, and when the doorbell rang just before five, I felt reasonably calm and collected.

Eileen was the first to arrive, and soon after her my four neighbours came in too. Comita and Eileen went into the kitchen to prepare the tea, and I was left sitting – rather awkwardly, I felt – with Ira, Lachryma, Pavida and Pudora.

I noticed with appreciation that they had, each in her own way, made efforts with their appearance. Ira had dispensed with her usual baggy jeans and was wearing a smart tailored suit in dark navy; Lachryma, perhaps in an attempt to disguise her chronically puffy cheeks, was rather garishly made up: she wore a purplish lipstick, mascara and a touch of rouge. Pudora and Pavida had both had their hair done – evidently by the same hairdresser, as their hairstyles were exactly the same.

So we sat, the five of us, formal and silent, while from the kitchen came the sound of laughter and the clattering of cups. I felt that it was incumbent upon me, as the hostess, to entertain my guests, but somehow the occasion seemed so significant that I couldn't find an appropriate conversational opening.

Finally, I cleared my throat and said formally:

"I am so pleased you're all coming this evening."

Four smiling faces turned towards me, and at that moment Eileen and Comita came into the room with the tea things.

"Here we are," Comita said, depositing a large tray on the table. To my surprise I saw that the tray bore a most elegant tea service – fine china with delicate floral decoration.

"Where has that come from?" I asked.

"It's yours!" said Comita. "We decided that you deserved something really nice, so we clubbed together and got you this."

I was too astonished to speak for a moment but eventually managed to stammer:

"Why, it's lovely, absolutely lovely, you really shouldn't have …"

A murmur of dissent ran round the room.

"Of course we should have!" Eileen said firmly. "It's time you had a few treats. And here's a special cake to mark the occasion of your return to the world."

From a tin she was carrying she produced a gateau – a flamboyant mixture of chocolate, nuts and cream.

Suddenly all was activity: tea was poured, cake cut, cups handed round, and there was an excited buzz of conversation.

"Are you nervous about this evening?" Pavida asked me.

"A little," I said. "But excited as well."

"Will there be a lot of people there?" Pudora asked.

"Probably," I told her.

"I hope they'll be appreciative," Lachryma said rather gloomily.

"Well," I said, "I can't help it if they're not. I've done my best."

"Of course you have!" said Ira. "If they don't like it, they can bloody lump it."

"Well, I'm glad you'll all be there," I said again.

"We'll be there all right," said Comita. "We'll be with you all the way."

"Yes," echoed Eileen. "We'll see you successfully outed."

I continued to feel reasonably confident while we were taking tea, but when the moment came for us to set off, a sudden doubt crept in. At the back of my mind was the experience I had had on the previous occasion I had gone to give my lecture. I still remembered the impassable footman who had declared me missing.

Surely, though, he wouldn't dare do that now, not with all my friends there around me. They knew I wasn't missing, they knew I was due to speak. They had done so much to help me prepare for the occasion – I must do them proud now.

On a sudden impulse, as the taxis drew up outside and we prepared to leave the house, I picked up the Blue Vase from its customary place on the table and stuffed it into my bag.

11.50 p.m.

Only a few more minutes left of today. Only a few more lines to write.

When the taxis drew up at the entrance to the Literary Society, I looked out anxiously for the footman. He was nowhere to be seen, but an usher, who closely resembled him, was standing by the door. Dark-suited and pompous-looking, he was holding a list in his hands and, as I mounted the steps with my 'entourage', he stepped forward officiously to greet us.

"Good evening. Your tickets, please."

"Good evening," I responded. "I'm the guest speaker, Dr Wentworth, and these ladies are all with me."

"Oh," the man said, slightly taken aback. "I'm so sorry, Dr Wentworth – it's such a long time since we've seen you. I didn't recognise you at first. This way, please. The President of the Society has asked me to take you and your party directly to the Byron Room where he will entertain you with refreshments."

As we followed the usher through the main hall where the guests were assembling, I saw heads turning in our direction and heard people murmuring my name. I felt overwhelming relief. I was here, I was recognised, I was Emily Wentworth!

At 7 p.m. I took my place on the platform in the lecture hall. The room was filled to capacity and there was an expectant buzz of talk. My six friends were sitting prominently in the front row, nodding and smiling at me. I felt calm and confident as the President made his introductory remarks:

"Ladies and Gentlemen," he said, "I am delighted to welcome our speaker, Dr Emily Wentworth, who is back with us after a long illness. Her talk this evening is entitled 'Layers of Meaning'."

As I stood up to address the audience, I suddenly recalled that I had with me in my bag the Blue Vase. Carefully taking it out, I held it aloft and then placed it before me on the table.

"Ladies and Gentlemen," I began, "please, regard this vase – which may, at first sight, appear to be an empty vessel ..."

THE END

About the Author

Sylvia Moody is a Classicist, psychologist, writer and translator. Her non-fiction books range from a lay person's guide to Ancient Greek philosophy to a series of books on dyslexia in adulthood. She has also written short stories and poetry for both adults and young children. She lives in London but has spent many years in Greece; her translations from Modern Greek include history and biography, museum guides, catalogues for art exhibitions, short stories and poetry.

Printed in Great Britain
by Amazon.co.uk, Ltd.,
Marston Gate.